Destiny's War

Part 1: Saladin's Secret

PYRAM KING

<u>DESTINY'S WAR</u>
PART 1: SALADIN'S SECRET
PART 2: ASSASSIN AWAKES

www.destinyswar.com

ISBN-13: 978-1-7341358-0-0 (print)
ISBN-13: 978-1-7341358-1-7 (eBook)

Library of Congress Control Number: 2019916628

Cover design by Ebook Launch
Artwork by Daniela Irizarry

First printed edition 2020

Pyram King LLC
151 Calle San Francisco
San Juan, PR 00901

For Jace Magellan King,
a true explorer and adventurer

Contents

Acknowledgments

A special thanks to Todd Merer. He provided the key that unlocked the door. Daniela Irizarry provided magic and vision that brought the story to life.

Thanks to my content editor, Allister Thompson, who spent time reviewing as well as challenging my ideas and providing an objective perspective. Another thank you to my copy editor, Stephanie Stringham, who tirelessly corrected my work and correctly interpreted my meaning.

Most importantly, thank you to my family and friends. Your support, thoughts, and willingness to listen were the encouragement I needed to see this through.

Introduction

Destiny's War is a series of novellas. The story is a fictional account based on the diaries of Francis Marion Jäger and weaves together two worlds: the Great War of the early twentieth century, and the ancient world. Part 1: Saladin's Secret, leads us into the war and the mystery of Saladin's secret.

Writing *Destiny's War* was a unique journey of exploration of history, requiring research and detective work. I have provided sketches, an index, and endnotes for those interested in the history, people, and places. Unfortunately, there is not enough room to provide all of this information; as such, additional information can be found on the website www.destinyswar.com.

The Middle Eastern theater of the Great War (World War I), while not as extensively covered as the European theater, was a critical part of the war, which shaped the future of the Middle East. A more deep-rooted history—ancient history from thousands of years ago—is woven into this story: Saladin, Templars, Sinān, and Kahn, whose actions have laid the foundation for future events.

History does not consist of isolated events but of a series of cause and effect. We are often unaware of how an event today may influence the future; there is much truth to the law of unintended consequences and how far into the future the effects of our actions may reach.

If you would like to experience and visualize the Middle East during the Great War, I highly recommend viewing David Lean's epic movie, *Lawrence of Arabia*.

To find out more about *Destiny's War*, please visit www.destinyswar.com.

Setting

The Great War has raged for almost four years since the Archduke's assassination.[1] One man, one bullet, one death, caused nations to collide in chaos and felled people by the millions.

This story begins with a boy far from home in a foreign land, in a theater of conflict mired in confusion. It is a place of peoples and history woven together by stories passed through time in the oral tradition, creating a patchwork of myths. Lost are the parchments and scrolls bringing light to the truth.

The Desert Sea has laid waste to man and history, far more than any war ever could. It is the Desert Sea that plays a significant role in this story, the canvas on which the story is painted.

One man's death was the singularity that spun the world into conflict. One boy may prevent the world's destruction.

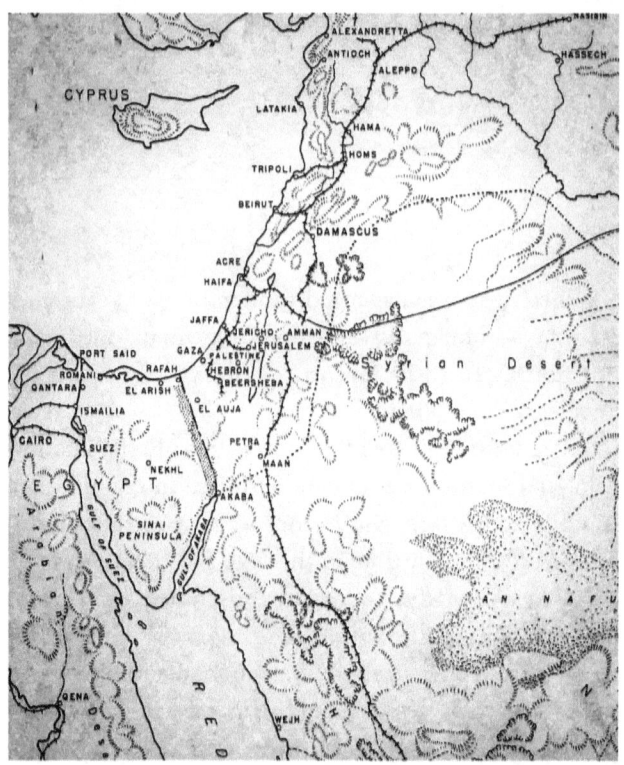

1 Map: Middle East Theater World War I (c. 1917)

Syria, August 1917

The acrid stink of gunpowder fills my nose, and makes my eyes water. My lungs are raw. My ears ring, muting the cracks of gunfire and screams. I am unable to process what is happening; I have no muscle memory for battle.

I stand, frozen, staring at the man I have just shot. The blood is darker than I remember. Memories flood in, of a deer I killed: the deer's eyes, its gaze somehow forgiving, as life faded. The memory seems so far off, a lifetime ago. The man's eyes are the same … life begins to fade.

No, he is not a man but a youth, not much older than myself. His hand grips an amulet around his neck. His lips quiver. A prayer?

"Mare!" a distant voice calls out.

I am Mare, I remember … or used to be, before I killed a man … a boy. What was his life like? His dreams? I bend down, unclench his fingers. The amulet hangs from a rawhide string without knowing why I rip it free.

"*Mare!*" The voice is louder.

A hand grabs my shoulder. I wheel around, raising my rifle, ready to strike. I quickly lower my guard when I see it is my friend, my only friend in this hell on earth.

"We have to go. Now!" His voice is panic-stricken.

Still dazed, I nod. I look back at the boy I just killed, my first kill. Flies are buzzing in the blood. I slip the amulet into my pocket. The dark blood pools, ready to touch the tip of my boot—the thin line between life and death.

ACT 1:
SHADOWS
OF AZRAQ

KANTARA, EGYPT,
JULY 1917

CHAPTER 1

Kantara

El Qantara, or Kantara as the English call it, is south of Port Said and north of Suez. It is the busiest city in all of Egypt. Straddling both sides of the Suez Canal, it is the central supply depot for all the Allied forces.

On any given day, ANZACs bloodied from Gallipoli[2] and looking for a fight invade Kantara before shipping off to another front. Of course, the Brits believe Kantara their base of operations, and visiting Kantara during their downtime does wonders to keep the ANZACs and Brits at bay from a bloody thumping they would give each other, after one too many pints of ale.

El Qantara is also the collection depot for too many bodies returning from the front. A while back, the British started a cemetery outside of town, as the parade of bodies continued. I ventured to the graveyard after the war first broke out in early '15, almost two years ago, after a young soldier I traveled with on my first reporting assignment to the front fell in battle. He was not much older than me, and I accompanied the body back to Kantara. I have forgotten his name as I have witnessed more soldiers falling in battle. Now I remember him merely

3

as Seventeen, not because of his age but because he happened to be seventeenth buried at the cemetery. Today, well over five hundred are buried here; I vow never to return.

The Brits have recently given the Turks a bloody bashing across the Sinai to make up for a most embarrassing defeat during the Siege of Kut,[3] which the Brits prefer to call the Defense of Kut. Perhaps now the body count at the cemetery will slow.

Kantara lives for the war, and when this war ends, so will Kantara. Kantara is not a real city; it is a staging area for soldiers coming back or heading to the front. You can feel death in the air. After two days, I need to take my leave. I have come to collect my stipend for my stories about the front, at the makeshift London paper office. *Closed for lunch,* reads the handwritten sign; I will come back later.

I sneak into the British officers' mess to have some fresh lemonade and, of course, read up on the news from the rest of the world. The bartender has let me enter the servants' door in the back alley. I take my usual seat at the end of the bar and enjoy my lemonade in peace, listening to newly arrived officers pontificate on the war effort. They regurgitate headlines from the very paper I write for as if they have grasped an understanding of this war. They speak loudly for all to hear, as their pent-up excitement for battle is barely containable.

The seasoned officers, with eyes hollow from battle, remain quiet and simply nod. They have their own private term for these new officers: *fresh meat.* They know most of the fresh meat will be dead by year's end and that those who survive will learn a vital lesson: *No one knows why we are here.*

This is the cycle I see play out time and time again in the officers' mess. Oh, Kantara, the purgatory for soldiers, a waypoint to death's door. I hope never to return.

The Desert Sea has become the canvas for this theater of war, soaking up the blood of the dead and sucking the souls from the living. The desert hungers for fresh meat, and when the hot lead and cold steel of battle does not kill, the desert does.

I do not notice how quiet the officers' mess has become until the smell of camel fills my nose. My eyes catch a glimpse of a once-white robe, now stained and dirty. I turn to see the piercing blue eyes, sun-bleached hair, and darkened face weathered by sun and toiled by war. His parched lips utter a whisper to the bartender. "Lemonade."

I have heard the talk—the rumors—but to see him ... Now I understand the fascination; I cannot put it into words. The rumors do not do his presence justice. There is a quiet calm about him, but I feel he could move mountains if he commanded it. He lives in his own world, figuratively and judging by his dress literally.

He turns toward me, raising his glass of lemonade, and I return the gesture of silent respect. After offering a becoming smile, a quick wink, he drinks the entire glass of lemonade in one go. He nods to the bartender, places the empty glass carefully on the bar, turns, and exits as quickly as he entered.

Rumors have spread that he took Akaba by land with a small band of Bedouins on horseback and camel. He must have crossed al-Houl, a section of desert considered unpassable even by Bedouins. If true, it is a miracle. The British failed to take Akaba by sea, and no one dares try by land.

Several officers have frozen, staring at him as he leaves. A few glance at me, and I nod in recognition of their attention. Too many of them, I will not see again, I know; many will never return home. But not him, the blue-eyed, blonde Bedouin; he will survive this war, perhaps become a legend if the rumors are true.

I keep to myself and enjoy the rest of my lemonade. Occasionally, some fresh meat will join me at the bar; today is no different.

"Looks as if everyone has just seen a ghost," comes the loud crack of a highborn English accent near me.

"Ey?" I turn to the young British officer.

"What's with everyone?"

"He was just here enjoying a lemonade." I return to my own drink.

"The general?"

"Lawrence."[4]

"Who?" Clearly, the young officer is another piece of fresh meat and has not heard the rumors about Lawrence. Taking notice of my drink, he adds, "That scrumpy doesn't look too good."

"It's lemonade with a touch of fruit paste—tamarind, I think." A while back, I traded for tamarind from the far east of Arabia; a Bedouin friend often brought the fruit paste to me for a shiny penny, knowing my fondness for it.

2 July 1917 Lawrence, Kantara – F.M. Jäger (c. 1917)

Without asking, the officer pulls up a stool and sits next to me. "Tamarind? Wog-talk. It's all gibberish."

"Actually, I'm fluent in Arabic."

He laughs. "Are you now? And I'm the man in the moon. Now empty your cup of that dirty water and have a proper stiff with me. Name's Benjamin Wright; just plain Ben does the trick. And you are …?"

"Mare. My friends call me—"

Another hearty laugh as he pours me a drink. " 'f a bloke called me Mare, I'd knock his head and tell him my name's Stallion."

His laugh is infectious. I smile. "Mare's short for Marion—"

"Another womanly name. Say, you're not a poof?"

My smile vanishes. "I'm named after my mother's great-uncle," I reply, bristling. "Fellow named Francis Marion.[5] You Brits called him the Swamp Fox because he outthought and outfought you at every turn of a minor event called the American Revolution. Ever hear of it?"

"Indeed, I have, my Yankee Doodle friend. Lost an ancestor or two in it. Perhaps at the hand of yours. Ah, well. War's war. Let's drink to it, Mare."

Ben swallows his drink in a gulp. I try to do the same, but the stuff is so intense, I erupt into a fit of coughing. A couple of fresh officers at the bar laugh, but Ben silences them with a glare.

With a twinkle in his blue eyes, Ben refills both our cups. "Drink hearty, Mare. It may be a while until our next opportunity."

"Why do you say that?"

"Tomorrow I head out to Rafah, to join up with Second British Battalion." He pauses, then adds, "The Camel Corps,"[6] as if I have no clue. He continues, "Be serving under Captain Wilson of the Fifth Company."

"That's Major Bassett's Battalion,"[7] I reply.

"Why yes, it is. Bassett's raid on Nekhl is already legendary."[8]

"Oh, is it, now?" Little does Ben know; I saw this supposedly legendary raid firsthand. I was with Captain Wilson's Camel Company, reporting from the front during the raid. It is a small world.

"Why, yes, it's even written up in the London papers."

"Here's to the London papers!" I raise my glass barely off the table, in the weakest of efforts, thinking my story, well received in London, is barely making a pound sterling, which I must beg for. No doubt, Ben probably read about the raid on the ship from London on his way to Kantara.

"So, you can ride a camel?" I ask.

"Went to Abbassia,[9] learned what I needed. Rode horses as a boy. I'm meant for the cavalry. Anyways, we're headed to battle. No doubt." He raises his cup. "To action, Mare!"

We clink cups and drink. This time I do not cough, although I am perplexed. Here is another young man, eager to see battle, no doubt, but on a camel. I am surprised Ben is so excited, but his khakis are new, so perhaps he has just arrived in the theater of this little-known part of the Great War in which the British Empire is engaging the Ottomans.[10]

"Say, Mare, what's a Yank doing here with His Majesty's Army?"

"My employer is a London newspaper who pays me a pittance to dispatch news from the war, but Europe and Gallipoli are where all the news is. Not much interest here. Except for your Camel Corps." I wink.

Ben looks shocked. "That was your story?"

"Yup, rode with Captain Wilson myself and even took the photo. I'm just the news dispatch, don't get any credit for it." I never receive credit for any of the stories. The pompous English reporter who never leaves his office in Kantara takes the credit. "Now … unfortunately, my stipend is overdue, so perhaps I'm unemployed. I wish you the best of luck in Rafah, or wherever you're headed. Me, I'm headed back to London or somewhere."

"Without a job?"

"Seems so." I grab my rucksack, place a penny on the bar, and give the bartender a nod.

"Wait! Why not accompany the battalion? Once at the front, you'll have stories galore. If the fogies in London are not interested, you could write a book." This stranger seems to have taken a shine to me, which always seems to be the case with the fresh-faced boys arriving at war. I have seen it before, a young man seeking desperately for a friend in this foreign land brimming with the horrors of war.

"A novelist on a camel? I write—I should say *wrote*—for a newspaper, about this part of the war no one else is interested in covering. I hear there's an opening for a cargo master running goods up the Nile."

I begin to walk out, and Ben follows.

"Cargo master on the Nile? Come now, you've ridden a camel and already know Major Bassett and the Camel Corps." He can see I am not buying it. "My father's friends with the brigadier general." As if that will change my mind.

I have grown tired of the battlefield, and I have a sinking feeling Ben will become another number, like Seventeen. I will not—cannot—begin making friends with another young man just to see him die. War rots the soul.

I stop and turn. "Ben, I've ridden my share of camels and seen too many a fine man fall. … I'll think about it."

"Don't take too long; we leave by train to Rafah in a couple of hours." He waves as I take my leave.

I head a few streets down, to the London paper office to collect my fee and get word of a possible assignment. Although the pound sterling awaits, my services are no longer in need, as I expected, and to my chagrin. The English reporter in Kantara has left for London, perhaps to a hero's welcome for his excellent reporting from the front. The thought of him taking credit for my stories give me pains, but not so long as to generate genuine concern. I have other plans, and they do not involve writing for the London paper. Perhaps I will take Ben up on his offer.

I quickly head back to the officers' mess. If Ben is there, I will join him on the way to Rafah.

CHAPTER 2

To Azraq

I lean out the window in a failed effort to cool myself and to clear my nose of the putrid smell that fouls the train: soldiers, loaded for battle and heading to the front, most not having bathed in days. The sun's heat turns the train into an oven, baking soldiers for hours. It is a ripe, foul odor.

I sit down on a hard bench. The leather cushions have seen far better days, before the war. My ass is in more pain from the bench than from riding a camel for days, and my sweat-soaked shirt sticks to the leather. The haphazard bouncing on the rails across the desert has me missing the flowing movement of a camel on the Desert Sea.

What am I doing? I ask myself, though I know the answer: Heading back into war, no longer as a reporter. The only job I will have is to escort another body back from the front.

I shake the thought from my head. Have I become numb to the war over the years? Did Ben convince me, or am I just looking for a place to hide awhile? A perplexing position. I must be mad, but I feel I need to be here.

"Yank!" a rough voice calls out.

"Hey, Yank! I'm talking to you!" He is a British soldier sitting across the aisle, looking battle-scarred and with the stink of drink about him.

I try to pretend not to see him, but too late. I made eye contact.

His unshaven weathered face and bloodshot eyes show he cares naught for life anymore. Confrontation is the only way he can communicate. He has been in the theater for far too long.

"Whatcha doin' on our train? Come to fight the Turks?" It is a sad effort, but he continues forth. "Whars da rest of ya doughboys? Let'in' us do your fight'n'?" He gives a weak elbow jab to the soldier sitting next to him, perhaps to garner support. The jabbed fellow gives a mindless nod and then returns to staring out the window.

Ben snaps at the weathered soldier, "He ain't into any argy-bargy over it! He's a reporter for the London paper."

It is enough; the angry soldier turns away and gives me no more bother. Perhaps a few months earlier, the burly man would have weighed another stone[11] and been ready for a tumble, yet now he is, like many others on the train, a shell of his former self. Sadly, he can muster only enough talk to attempt to save his dignity.

Talk ceases as the click-clack-click-clack of the train becomes hypnotic. A warm, calm blankets the train as we wander across the desert. The emptiness draws one in, causing one to quickly become lost in one's own mind.

I look across the aisle. The weathered soldier, lost to his own dream, his eyes dead, stares out into the nothingness of the desert.

3 Train to Azraq July 1917 –[from Kantara to Rafah] -
F.M. Jäger (c. 1917)

A strange land, a stranger war. Most have no idea why they are killing or even whom they are killing. Ours is a train full of soldiers lost to humanity, shell-shocked, tired, sent off to a place to kill or die. Most will be forgotten in time.

We arrive at Rafah, the last stop on the Sinai Military Railway, as the hot sun begins to set. They are laying track as far as I can see. Gaza may be next, perhaps even Jerusalem.

The makeshift train station is full of the typically ordered chaos conducted by the British. Soldiers lumber as directed by officers; local merchants sell worthless trinkets, Bedouin knives, and the highly sought-after Turkish army souvenirs collected off the dead. It is an ugly affair after a desert battle, nomad scavengers quickly arriving like vultures, rifling the corpses in the desert for boots, ammunition, weapons, and trinkets. They strip bodies bare in many cases. A sharp knifepoint pops a tooth out if it wears a crown of gold. Fingers are chopped off for rings, and necklaces are yanked from necks. What they are not able to use, the scavengers sell to local merchants to sell at bazaars, realizing the fresh meat arriving for war hunger for tokens off dead enemy soldiers. I am sure somewhere in the north, the same nomads sell trinkets of British soldiers from the same battlefield.

I wonder is the merchant selling a trinket off the dead also admiring potential trinkets on the living? How many trinkets from dead soldiers have returned to the battlefield with their new owners, then been collected off fresh dead and resold in the bazaars? It is disgusting, but one must admire the nomads' ingenuity and tenacity. The nomads have survived for centuries in the most inhospitable conditions, and now two foreign powers have turned their land into a killing field, supplying a bloody marketplace.

"Lively now! Step-to!" yells the sergeant.

"Lieutenant Benja—," Ben tries to identify himself. He cannot finish.

"On you go, laddie, move!" snaps the sergeant, ignoring Ben's formal salute.

A young soldier comes pushing through the crowd, calling, "Lieutenant Wright! Lieutenant Wright!"

Ben hails his attention, and the young soldier salutes. He is to lead Ben to Captain Wilson. The Fifth Company has recently moved northeast of the Dead Sea to the ruins at Qasr Azraq. It is going to be a far and challenging ride, and not a safe one. We will have to cross the Hejaz railway,[12] which is the Ottoman railway from Damascus to Medina and a major supply route. It will be well guarded.

The soldier is not expecting me, so Ben quickly explains that I am a reporter and am to accompany him. The soldier shrugs; his mind is on the journey back north, back into enemy territory.

Just beyond the military's makeshift train station, I secure a camel from a Bedouin unloading his caravan. The camel is beautiful and has a happy demeanor, which is rare for a camel. She has a funny tuft of hair sticking up next to her ear, so I name her Tuff. She is happy to find a new master; the Bedouin caravans frequently overburden camels, which breaks their spirit.

* * *

We will ride all night and hope to make Azraq, in enemy territory, in a few days.

History is repeating itself; the Allied forces are engaging in the ancient pincer movement, enveloping the enemy from two sides, a strategy used hundreds of times from Alexander the Great to Napoleon. Damascus is the prize. The first claw of the pincers comes from the south as the Allies move north across the Sinai. The second claw comes from the east, as the Allies press up the Euphrates River valley through Mesopotamia. There is no escape for the enemy to the west; the coast of the Mediterranean has a fleet of British warships ready to pound it.

The ruins at Azraq sit in the middle of the area below the two claws of the Allied pincers. To the west of Azraq, the Allied forces push north. To the east is the Desert Sea, which must be crossed to reach the Euphrates.

Azraq is likely too remote to garner any attention from the enemy. The Fifth Company is on a long-range reconnaissance mission, perhaps to be the eyes of the Allied forces. I wonder how far the company will travel into enemy territory. It must be a secret mission, certainly a dangerous one. Maybe Ben is right and this could be the making of a great story, yet I have an uncomfortable feeling this may be far more than I bargained for.

* * *

It takes us five days to ride from Rafah to Azraq. We cross the Hejaz railway far south of Amman, away from civilization. We see not a single living soul; we are on the edge of the Desert Sea, Ben's first time in the vast nothingness.

4 Tuff - F.M. Jäger (c. 1917)

Ben is relieved when we arrive in Azraq to see fellow soldiers, tents, and a small military post snuggled in the ruins. For him, the military routine is a sign of life and perhaps security. Ironically, it pains me to see ancient ruins commandeered by soldiers who have no knowledge of and therefore no respect for their significance. These are important historical places, many still holding secrets. Perhaps my repeated readings of Burton's[13] travels and working on archeological sites before the war have tainted me.

We enter the ruins. The late-afternoon sun beats down on the ancient arches, casting a long shadow. They morph into a black claw grasping at lumbering soldiers passing beneath them ... an ominous sight, a memory I shall never forget.

A small sign adorns the entrance to an ancient building: **2-BAT HQ**. I follow Second Lieutenant Benjamin Wright into the headquarters of Second Battalion.

The command-post aide, an older enlisted man, is focusing on some papers at his desk, ignoring Ben and me.

"Second Lieutenant Benjamin Wright, reporting for duty!" Ben gives a snapping salute and a click of his heel.

"Tish tosh, what's this noise about?" asks a voice from the other room.

Major Bassett walks in, followed by an older, higher-ranking officer. The major has a rock for a face, and the sun has darkened it. His uniform is a little loose and threadbare. The aide jumps to attention. Ben salutes, this time with a stomp of his feet ... a slightly rich English military tradition that I never have quite figured out.

5 Azraq 1917 - F.M. Jäger (c. 1917)

"Ben? Benjamin Wright? Is that you?" the older officer inquires.

"Sir, yes, SIR!"

"At ease, Lieutenant. Please, come in," the older officer states calmly.

Ben lowers his salute as the aide stays at attention, staring off toward the wall. The major casts a smart look toward the aide, which reads, *I am watching you.*

I follow Ben and the other officers into what seems to be the command office.

"Well, well, what a fine officer you have turned out to be," the older officer says calmly. Ben stands at attention without responding, seemingly at a loss for words.

"Ben, please have a seat. How's your father?"

Before Ben can answer, the major interrupts. "I know you; you are ..." He has taken notice of me for the first time and is staring.

"This is my close dear friend, Francis Marion Jäger. His friends call him Mare. He's a reporter for a London paper, reporting on the war effort." Ben seems to feel safe to stick his neck out for me and does so in a natural way.

"Yes, I remember now, you were with Captain Wilson at the raid. Well, I see. We, of course, will make your stay comfortable, I should also like to hear news from London, if you care." The major seems far more at ease after Ben's explanation. "Please have a seat."

"Francis Marion? I shall hope you are on our side this time," the older officer quips with a tone of English wit.

I nod respectfully. "I'm at your service. While I'd hope to do my ancestry proud, I'm sure he's rolling over in his grave."

The older officer laughs and smiles, approving of my parry. "Yes, yes, right, you are. Please join us."

Ben and I sit down across from the major and older officer.

"Ben, I had no idea you were assigned to one of my battalions," the older officer begins.

Embarrassingly, I only just realize that am in the presence of Brigadier General Smith,[14] commander of the Imperial Camel Corps, a very well-respected and trusted general of the King's Army. I certainly feel like a fool, not recognizing him at first. Ben did say he knew the general; little did I give him credit.

The general continues, "How's your father?"

"Sir, he's well, and he sends you his regards. He wishes he could be here serving with you again."

"Your father is the finest officer I've ever served with. He's sorely missed, and I could use his sage wisdom fighting these Turks."

"I assume you're serving with Captain Wilson; I'm told a lieutenant has been dispatched to serve for one of his sections," states the major.

"Yes, sir, I'm to report to Captain Wilson." Ben pauses, then continues in a hushed whisper, "I have an important communiqué to deliver to the major." Ben opens his shirt and pulls from it a sealed envelope, which he hands to the major as if it contains top-secret war plans.

The major immediately opens the letter and reads it carefully. Then he nods, handing the message to the general. "Thank you, Lieutenant. Captain Wilson will be here shortly; he's with a patrol which had a run-in, I hear with some Bedouins who may have been spying for the Turks."

The general glances at the letter and nods before saying, "Interesting, Major, and as I expect. Oppenheim, who once led the German Intelligence Bureau,[15] whereabouts unknown. Seems the Germans are searching for him as well."

"Sir, I thought the message strange. I believe von Schowingen replaced him several years ago?"

"Yes, now Mittwoch is the head of German intelligence. The point: We have lost track of bloody Max, and I shall not have this boche ramshackle the Camel Corps!" The general is obviously irritated with this Max, I reflect, considering that the name sounds familiar.

"Excuse me, sir, do you mean Max von Oppenheim,[16] the German archeologist?" I ask. It cannot be the same, surely.

"Why yes, he was an archeologist before the war. Working on a dig a few hundred miles north for some time. There was a bit of a flap about it; we had our own expedition close by. In fact, I believe Lieutenant Lawrence was on the expedition." The general shakes his head. "Even fighting over ruins in the desert."

"I met Oppenheim briefly," I state. "I was sent to fetch some kit left by the English archeologist. He's a dark fellow, obsessed. Plumb crazy, if you ask me."

The general's eyebrows rise as he hears my assessment. "Never had the misfortune to meet the fellow. Hope I never shall." He turns to the major. "It's not like the Germans to pull an effective man from the field. It worries me the Germans are looking for him as well. I would like to know what Oppenheim is up to. I do *not* want him mucking about as we push our forces north. He has caused us enough grief over the years."

6 Brigadier Smith - F.M. Jäger (c. 1917)

"Yes, sir. I'll make sure to send word as soon as we learn of his whereabouts," responds the major.

The general looks at me. "Mr. Jäger, may I have a word with you? I wish to ask you a few questions about London."

"I'm not sure if I can be of help, but I'll try."

"Well, it's a delicate matter, a personal one, if you don't mind." The general is clearly attempting to politely inform the major that this is a private matter.

I have not the foggiest of ideas about what the general wishes to engage with me about.

"Of course, sir." The major rises, signaling to Ben with a nod. They both stand to attention, salute, spin, and march out of the room.

"What may I do for you, sir?" I ask the general.

"You're acquainted with a friend of mine, Ms. Bell.[17] Am I correct?" he replies.

I quickly glance at my watch, comforted by its presence. The small print, **SIGNAL CORPS,** underneath **OMEGA** on the face of the watch is a reminder of whom I serve. The watch was a gift from Ms. Bell the year before. "You're my personal signal corps," she said amusingly, referencing the print on the watch's face. After the war had broken out, I had been a reporter for the London paper for a few months, riding with the British troops and reporting from the front. In the officers' mess, she had requested my presence. Ms. Bell is the only commissioned woman in the theater, well respected and with very close ties to the Crown. She operates an intelligence network. She summoned me because she desired someone not in the military to be her eyes and ears on

7 Ms Bell - F.M. Jäger (c. 1916)

the front. My working for the London paper provided a perfect cover. I am a civilian, an American, a reporter, and I speak Arabic and German. I was to remain at my job and report directly to her. I meet with her a few times a year. She once called me the Kim to her Kipling.[18] I guess I am her spy.

I glance at the general, trying to formulate a response. "Yes, I'm acquainted with her. I had the pleasure of meeting her for a story I was writing."

"Come now, Francis…" He pauses and leans in carefully. In a hoarse whisper, he utters, "The lightly burdened shall be saved."

Ms. Bell's passphrase. If someone is to meet with me, it is what they will say. It is the first of a series of Bedouin proverbs, not often spoken in English. If the series is correctly spoken in order, it means the person is a trusted friend of Ms. Bell.

"Truth may walk through the world unarmed," I respond properly.

"He who shares my bread and salt is not my enemy," he responds correctly. "Now our introductions have concluded, may I ask your interest in the Camel Corps and the Fifth Company directly?"

"I went to report to Ms. Bell since I was recently discharged by the London paper. She was away on official business when I met Benjamin at the officers' mess. He invited me to travel along north with him. I thought it an opportunity, rather than waiting in Kantara, which I do not find pleasant."

"I see. I assumed Ms. Bell had sent you. We have taken the Sinai and will be pressing the Turks at Gaza soon. We must not allow the Turks to cut us off from the east. I have given orders to the Fifth Company to move deep into Syria, an advance operation to monitor and potentially raid supply lines. This is a sensitive mission and a dangerous one." He leans in closely, touches his nose, and gives me a nod. "Not one for the books."

I know what he means; it is a secret mission, and there is probably more here than he is sharing with me. "Excellent, sir. Is my presence going to be a bother?"

"Actually, quite the contrary. Your presence is most fortuitous. We are about to plan the Fifth Company's mission, and I would like you to join us. Your knowledge of the area may be of use."

"Anything I can do, sir."

"Now make sure to tell Benjamin—as he will certainly ask—that I was interested in obtaining the score on the match at Lord's.[19] I actually have a friendly wager on our boys giving the ANZACs and South Africans a bit of stick."

"Yes, sir. I actually read up on the match at Kantara."

"Pray tell, I had no idea. The score, out with it," demands the general.

"It was a draw. Australia and South Africa took the lead, but England came back strong to finish in a draw."

"Very good, very good. Now I have matters to attend." He rises and straightens his jacket, then places his cap on his head. I follow him out the door into the reception area.

The general turns to Ben. "Ben, I'm so glad to see you and glad you're with us."

"Sir!" the major fairly shouts, snapping a salute. As Ben follows in a similar style, I nod to the brigadier general.

"Major, I'll be back in short order for our scheduled briefing, and then I must be off." The general returns the salute, turns, and walks out the door.

"Second Lieutenant, I'll call the sergeant to take you to your quarters. There's a double room if you do not mind sharing with your friend Mr. Jäger."

"I prefer Mare," I mention.

"Please join us for dinner in the officers' mess. The boys would care to hear news from home," the major states firmly.

I follow Ben out of the command post. As the general predicted, Ben is eager for details about our private meeting. "So, what did the general want to discuss that's so private?"

"I think he is embarrassed to admit; he has a wager on the cricket match at Lord's and wanted to know if I have the score since I work for the paper."

"Really, the general wagering on a cricket match? Never knew generals did that sort of thing," Ben says, sounding astonished.

"I'm sure he also puts on his own trousers," I joke.

Ben slaps me on the back, and we share a good laugh.

CHAPTER 3

Al-Ḥashāshīn

I settle my belongings in the room with Ben before returning to the makeshift battalion HQ.

"Sir?" the enlisted man at the desk asks, recognizing me.

"I'm here to see Brigadier General Smith."

"Is he is expecting you?"

"I believe he is."

Major Basset steps into the room and says, "Ah, Marion, please come in. We have been expecting you." I give a quick nod and smile to the enlisted man and follow the major into the larger room beyond.

The well-worn wooden table in the center of the room has a large map spread across it. At the bottom of the map is the tip of the Sea of Galilee. At the top is the city of Hama, with Damascus right in the middle. I have been to Hama, and even farther north, before the war, when I traveled with my Bedouin friend.

Brigadier General Smith and Captain Wilson, whom I recognize, stand at the table. Captain Wilson gives me a friendly smile; I have not seen him since the raid.

Brigadier General Smith says in a welcoming tone, "Mr. Jäger, we are sending Fifth Company north of Damascus. This is a reconnaissance mission, a sensitive one, as you can imagine. Moving men and equipment on camels is going to be a difficult task. We need to find a secure base of operations for Captain Wilson's men. I was wondering, since you have traveled in this area, if you have any suggestions?" I can feel the brigadier general's stare, as well as those of Major Basset and Captain Wilson.

I do not look up, instead focus on the map.

I lean over and stare, but it is not there. It is not on the map. I trace my finger along the lines marking the mountains north of Damascus, but I do not see it.

"Mr. Jäger?" Major Basset says inquisitively.

"Mar Musa. It's not on the map. It should be here," I say, pointing to a gap in the mountain range.

"Mar Mosa?" Captain Wilson has a habit of mispronouncing Arabic, which I learned when I was with him on the raid.

"Yes, old ruins in the mountains. A few monks stay there. It is like a monastery. It is on the east side of the mountains near the pass from Al-Nabek used by the Bedouins. The place is secret, known but to a few. Out of curiosity, I once visited with my Bedouin friend who knew about it."

"What is the terrain like? Fortifications, any other details?" the major asks.

"It is protected on three sides. There is a narrow mountain pass from the east leading to Mar Musa. The path is hard to find unless you know what to look for.

Mar Musa is hidden in a ravine in the mountains, almost impossible to find." I point to the east of Al-Nabek, on the other side of the marked mountain range.

I can see it in my mind's eye. "The terrain is steep. An old bridge suspends across a ravine to the south, leading to a small path running along the ridge to the west. I remember you can see well into the west from the top of the ridge. There are old buildings and ruins. I'm not sure if there is enough shelter for an entire company, but certainly 50 … maybe more. There were only a couple of monks the last time I visited. They were using one of the old ruins as a temple. The rest of the place was deserted."

"Very interesting. How far north of Damascus?" asks Brigadier General Smith.

"I would guess about fifty miles. I have made the journey in a day from Damascus, but it is a long ride, perhaps two days with a load."

The brigadier general nods. "How do you suggest we proceed to Mar Musa?"

"I would move north first." I look at the map and smile. "There!" I place my finger on the map. "The castle ruins of Salkhad. Two days north from here."

Salkhad is located south of the volcanic region of Druze. The castle ruins sit on a small plateau. Deraa is almost due east from the ruins. "You'll want to keep Deraa to your left flank. I suspect the British will take Deraa on its advance toward Damascus. Salkhad is where I would move Fifth Company. From there, you can strike the railway and Deraa in a day. You can also use it to stage an attack north to Damascus."

"We need to avoid Damascus," Major Basset states before turning to me. "Mr. Jäger, how do we get to Mar Musa if we are not to be seen?"

I stare at the vast area on the east side of the map, the Desert Sea. To the east of Salkhad lays the Rhube oasis, the last stop before crossing the desert. I put my finger on the oasis and trace a semicircle with my finger around Damascus and into the Desert Sea to Mar Musa. "There is only one way ... you must travel the Desert Sea if you wish to get to Mar Musa without the Turks noticing." There is no other way, and my suggestion is a dangerous one.

Captain Wilson, who was staring intensely at the map during our conversation, focuses on my finger. He is to lead his men deep into enemy territory and through the Desert Sea. We can feel the weight on his shoulders; if the Turks do not kill him, the Desert Sea might.

"Mr. Jäger, how much time, how long will it take?" There is urgency in the brigadier general's voice. Perhaps it is part of the British strategy to push forward against the Turks, yet I have a feeling there is far more at stake.

"From Salkhad? I can do it in three or perhaps four days, but I'm not sure about an entire company. Perhaps six to eight days. I would also send a patrol ahead. You do not know what may lie in wait for you in the Desert Sea, and there's also Mar Musa."

The major's tone becomes almost demanding. "Mar Musa? You said it's just a couple of monks!"

"That was before the war," I reply. "I have not been there in a couple of years or more. It's well protected and hidden, but I cannot say what it is like today."

8 Mar Musa - F.M. Jäger (c. 1914 - 1917)

Brigadier General Smith raises his hand to calm the situation. "Very well. Captain, select two rifle patrols from one of your sections. Once you reach Sal … Salk … Sa…"

"Salk-HOD, sir!" I look down at the map quickly, trying to ignore the fact that I just corrected the brigadier general. Hopefully, no one else has noticed.

"Right, Salk-HOD." He continues speaking to Captain Wilson. "Once Fifth Company's two patrols reach Salk-HOD, send a report back to Azraq. We want to move Fifth Company forward as quickly as possible. Immediately advance the patrols to the oasis and then to Mar Musa."

"Yes, sir!" the captain responds automatically.

"Captain, this mission is far too sensitive to leave it to chance. Divide the company: an advanced operation consisting of a rifle section and a machine-gun section, followed by a second rifle section as support with a Vickers[20]. Do not send your sections forward until you receive word from Mar Musa." The brigadier general contemplates the map carefully.

There is a seriousness in his voice as he speaks again—the weight of the decision he is making. I have the feeling he is none too keen to make it. "Major, pull from the other companies the additional camels and provisions Captain Wilson needs to support the remaining men of Fifth Company. The rest of Fifth Company will remain at Salk-HOD, and await further orders."

"Sir!"

The brigadier general glances up from the map. "Mr. Jäger, I would like you to join the patrol. You know the area and know where Mar Musa is. Without you, they will never find it. Get some rest; you leave tomorrow."

"Yes, sir," I reply, like one of his officers. It comes naturally.

I walk outside, contemplating my future. The moon is rising, casting a blue glow about the ruins, and the temperature is dropping. The stars are brighter here, away from the lights of Kantara. The breeze feels good.

What did I volunteer for? I ask myself. I did not volunteer; I was ordered. Perhaps the brigadier general, knowing my work with Ms. Bell, thinks I am in the service. I only pass on information; I am not a soldier. I am not formally part of the British Army.

"Mr. Jäger," the brigadier's voice is quiet behind me.

"Yes, sir?"

"I'm leaving before dawn. I'll inform Ms. Bell of your mission. I know this is not what you expected, but your service is needed, now more than ever."

I nod, not knowing what to say.

"Good luck and Godspeed." He respectfully offers his hand.

I stare briefly before accepting the hand. His grip is firm as his face becomes more somber. I feel he is saying good-bye, as he knows I may not make it.

"Sir, how do I get word to you?"

"In time. What will be, will be." He turns and hails a soldier, who snaps to attention to escort the brigadier general.

"Mr. Jäger, please join us in the mess," Major Basset calls from the entrance of battalion HQ, so I turn to join him and Captain Wilson to the mess hall.

"My wife is pleased with the fine article and very much cherished the picture. She said I have become the talk in Essex," Captain Wilson tells me, referring to the article I wrote for the London paper, making the Camel Corps a household term in London.

"Thank you for allowing me to ride with you," I tell him. I very much like Captain Wilson. "It was certainly a brilliant strategy, and I don't think the Turks had any idea what happened before it was too late."

"Have a seat. You must give us word from London," he says. Ben had joined us in the mess and I sit next to the captain and the major. A few other officers join us at the table.

As I share news from London, the officers hang on my every word. There is not much good news to tell, but seeing I am the only hope and salvation these unfortunate men have had in months, I do not want to pass on the report from the Western Front, or news of the mounting death tolls.

Although the war saw cricket almost come to an end in 1914, as few, if any, matches were played, I recently received news of a recent charity match at Lord's; the brigadier general had placed a friendly wager on the Brits giving the South African and ANZACs a bit of stick. Colin Blythe,[21] one of England's top players, had been at home on leave from the front and played for the British army-and-navy team against a combined Australian and South African team. The officers are excited to hear about the match, and I give them a play-by-play as best I can remember. The officers in the mess cheer and slap each other on the back. I had no idea how well-regarded

Blythe is among his countrymen. I see the gleam in their eyes at knowing that Blythe has again made England proud.

It is the best news they have heard in a long time, and an ease spreads through the mess hall, boosting morale. The major looks over to give me a smile and a nod; the news is just what the doctor ordered.

One officer begins sharing a story from a patrol he was on the other day. His patrol ran into a Bedouin group a couple of miles north of Azraq.

"The wog is saying some such nonsense over and over—Al Hash Sheen, AL Hash Sheen!"

"He's probably telling you to bugger off!" responds another officer, to the roar of laughter.

"Them wogs are always paddy," says another.

The British do not know the difference between Bedouin, Kurds, Turks, nomad scavengers, and the other peoples of the region. To the Brits, all were wogs. I am sure the locals cannot tell the difference between Brits, Americans, Germans, and French; we probably all look the same to them, too. When neither side bothers to know the other, knowing who the enemy is becomes as confusing as the reasons we are fighting

I lean over to Ben and whisper, "The Bedouin was saying 'assassins.' "

Captain Wilson looks at me. "What's that, Mr. Jäger?"

"The Bedouin was talking of assassins!"

"And just how do you know this?" Across the table, the officer telling the story sounds argumentative.

Major Bassett waves his hand as if to tell the officer to back off.

"Al-Ḥashāshīn[22] is Arabic for 'assassin.' " I feel all eyes glaring at me, and I no longer feel welcome. Quickly, I add, "I understand Arabic. It is one of the reasons London assigned me to report on the war." I assumed some of the officers know some Arabic, but it seems they do not.

"Assassins in the desert?" says one of them. The room again bursts into roaring laughter. With this release of tension, the officers' mess begins to clear. "Please join the captain and me in HQ when you're finished," Major Bassett says to me.

"Yer in the clinker," Ben says with a laugh as if I am in trouble.

I clear my setting and head to the battalion HQ.

CHAPTER 4

A Myth?

The oil lamps in the command room at HQ cast dark shadows on the wall. In the center of the room is the well-worn table on which lay the large maps we contemplated only an hour ago with the brigadier general.

"Please," Captain Wilson says, motioning me into the room.

"We intercepted some papers. Would you look at them?" the captain asks me.

He pulls what appears to be a scroll from a woven bag. I notice the woven bag is stained with blood, dark red, dried, and hardened.

"This is Bedouin," I marvel as I look at the bag. When he does not look up at me, I know that the patrol killed the Bedouin who tried to warn them about assassins. We are not at war with the Bedouin, and in fact, they are essential allies, but to the untrained Brit, all Arabs are the same. Echoing in my head is a phrase commonly heard among soldiers when they have too much to drink: *A good wog is a dead wog.*

The paper of the scroll is delicate, and I untie the cloth and leather wrapping carefully before unrolling the scroll equally carefully. It is written in Arabic, but I am unable to recognize some words. It reads like a poem or perhaps a story or prayer, undoubtedly ancient. A story of ancient battles, it seems.

"Well? Is there talk of these assassins?" The captain asks, staring at me thoughtfully.

"The Arabs invented assassins," I reply. "Even the word *assassin* comes from the Arabic word Ḥ*ashāshīn*."

I continue studying the scroll. When I see a name I recognize, I speak it softly to hear the words, "Shaykh al-Jabal."[23]

"Shake Al what? What are you bloody mumbling about?" Captain Wilson demands.

"Shaykh al-Jabal. It's a story, a myth of Shaykh al-Jabal." I can see I need to quickly translate, as I am losing the captain's patience. Major Bassett seems far more at ease.

" 'The Old Man of the Mountain' is what it actually translates to. He was the leader of the Assassins. People feared him, worshipped him, some believe he is a god. Some believe his spirit wanders the desert still."

"A god of assassins? These Arabs have a crude imagination. I expect no less from these heathens." The captain looks away, mumbling, "Bloody waste, fighting heathens who pray to assassin gods."

I realize I am holding a piece of history that the British Museum would envy. "Sir, this is a historical text, a valuable piece of history. If this is as old as I think it is, it can be 200 years old or even older. It seems to tell the story of Shaykh al-Jabal."

"I thought you said this is a story of a god. Are you telling me this Jabal character is a real person?" the captain asks. He does not seem to grasp what I have said.

"I don't know. But I do know his name is spoken with great care and respect. The Bedouins and all Arabs believe him to be a real person. The Bedouins seem to believe his spirit or ghost walks among us. They say a prayer before and after they speak his name and tell his story. They believe the prayer gives them protection from his spirit."

"Well, who's this bloody Jabal these Bedouins should be so scared of?" bellows the captain.

To my surprise, the major begins to speak as he steps toward the map table. "Sometime in the early twelfth century, a boy named Sinān arrives one day at the castle on the hill in Alamut, the home of the Assassins. He trains in the Assassins' crafts of spying, fighting, poisoning, and killing silently, and in the dark arts of mysticism, curses, and invocations. He becomes a SāḤib, which means 'master' in Arabic. His skills surpass those of his own master." Clearly, the Major knows the history of these parts.

Captain Wilson's look of astonishment is unmistakable.

"Yes, sir," I reply. "It's the story I heard from the Bedouin. They say Sinān grew strong and became the leader of the Assassins. He led his Assassin army to capture the small castle in Masyaf and made it his stronghold."

"Masyaf?" the captain interrupts.

"Yes, they're ruins a couple hundred miles north of here, south of Hama and north of Homs. It's near the mountains in the foothills." I point to an area of the map where Masyaf should be.

"So, the ruins were an Assassin fort, you say?" the captain asks, continuing to study the map.

"It's how the Bedouins describe it. They call the Battle of Masyaf 'the night death breathed.' Sinān and his Assassins killed every man, woman, and child in the castle without a single victim uttering a word; the only sound was their last breaths ... the night death breathed. Sinān turned the castle into a stronghold for his army of Assassins. He declared *Qiyamah*, which in Arabic means 'resurrection,' and created his own law, the law of the Assassins. Many feared him, and Masyaf became known as a place of great secrets and power. He became known as the Old Man of the Mountain. The story of his secret power spread, some believe he is a god."

Major Bassett stares at the shadows upon the wall. The shadows' dance on the wall reminds me of the first time I heard the stories of Masyaf. The Bedouins would share the myths of the castle on starry, moonless nights.

Unlike the major, Captain Wilson seems intent on the map and on plotting strategy.

Finally, Major Bassett breaks from his trance and nods his head. "The myth of Saladin and Sinān is well known. Saladin[24], the great ruler of Egypt, Syria, and most of North Africa who defeated the Christian Crusaders, is unable to conquer Masyaf and kill Shaykh al-Jabal, the Old Man of the Mountain, the leader, this god of the Assassins."

The major places his finger on the map, near the base of the mountains. "Saladin attacked and laid siege to the Assassin stronghold at Masyaf.[25] One night, a glowing light descended the hill from Masyaf into Saladin's encampment and disappeared into Saladin's tent. Saladin awoke from his sleep to see a glowing spirit of Shaykh

9 The old and the mountain Masyaf - F.M. Jäger (c. 1917)

al-Jabal leave his tent. Saladin found an assassin's dagger stuck into the table next to his bed with a note, which read he would die if he did not withdraw his troops by the next rising moon. Saladin left with his troops at sunrise the next morning, never to return. Saladin ordered his generals to protect Masyaf; no Christian, Jew, Arab, or living man should cross into the shadow of Masyaf. Word spread across the land, from the north of the Black Sea to the south of the Gulf of Aden, from the west of the Straits of Morocco to the east of the Gulf of Oman: 'Masyaf is under the protection of Saladin by order of death.' No man passed under the shadows of Masyaf for over 500 years."

"Sir, an intriguing and a rousing story, no doubt, but it *is* just a story," states Captain Wilson. He returns his focus to the map, his thoughts are on his men and the unknown dangers they face.

Major Bassett understands the significance of the story; it clearly strikes a chord with him as it does with me. Saladin is well known to anyone who has studied history, and I am sure the major, a well-educated officer, learned of the Crusades, and the feared name of Saladin, during his time at university. If Saladin was afraid of Sinān, the Old Man of the Mountains, there may be something more to Masyaf than meets the eye.

"Even today, many avoid Masyaf," I remind the major. "They believe it is cursed. Even the caravans avoid Masyaf's shadow."

Major Bassett nods as if indicating he is aware of this fact.

The room falls silent, and the captain slowly raises his eyes from the map to stare at me. Is he starting to believe in this myth?

We are indeed at the edge of the known world, and I am startled to realize that I am concerned about crossing this invisible barrier into the unknown. I shake my head to relieve myself of these thoughts.

"You seem to know a lot about this Old Man and Assassins," the captain says softly, his eyes never breaking contact with mine.

I refocus my attention to the map. "I traveled with some Bedouins, at night around the fire, they would tell stories about Saladin, the Assassins, and many other strange things in these lands."

"Do you believe in this … ?" His voice trails off, and I have the feeling he wishes to say something like "poppycock" to diminish the story's validity, but he now seems to take this history all too seriously.

"No, but they do." I nod toward the map. "And they are certainly fearful of something."

The major nods. He understands. "Fear can drive even the most God-fearing man unruly. These lands are not Christian. In Europe, we fight Christian men, but here, my soldiers' spirits have become rotten. Even Father Murphy seems uneasy in these lands."

I do not have the heart to tell the major or the captain that I have traveled the hajj, the pilgrimage to Mecca. I ran away from home at fourteen, which seems like a lifetime ago. I kept my mother's Bible with me after she passed away. My father read from it once, when we buried her, a year before I ran away from home. I never knew if Father believed in God. We did say a prayer before dinner, but perhaps it was for my mother's benefit while she was alive; the tradition ended with her death.

"Captain, send one of the patrols forward after it reaches Mar Musa. I'd like to know if the ruins at Masyaf are being used as a base of operations," Major Bassett commands.

"Yes, sir. I've assigned Lieutenant York of First Section and Lieutenant Richards of Second Section to lead the two patrols. I'll have Lieutenant Richards continue to Masyaf, then rendezvous back at Mar Musa. We'll assign someone to lead Second Section to Mar Musa." The captain turns to me. "I'd say about a week there and back from Mar Musa?"

"To Masyaf?" I thought about it. One had to continue north through the Desert Sea before heading west. It would be at least four days. "Perhaps four days from Mar Musa to Masyaf. You could get there and back in ten days."

The captain nods. "Very well."

"We need to know if the enemy is mounting an attack or using this as a base of operations. It would make sense, as the history and fear offer protection stronger than any walls." The major's voice echoes with quiet concern.

I can feel the major staring at me. I turn, knowing what he is about to say.

"You will travel with them to Masyaf!" he tells me as my eyes meet his.

My throat feels dry. I nod as the realization hits me: I am to travel into the unknown. This is no longer just a scout mission to find Mar Musa; I am to head to ruins of Masyaf. I am the only one who knows the way.

The memories of shadows cast from the arched ruins of Azraq, like black claws grasping at the soldiers, quickly come to mind and send a shiver down my spine.

ACT 2:
ROAD TO
MASYAF

CHAPTER 5

Long-Range Patrol

"Good morning" is all I say to Ben the next day. I am not in the mood to talk and want to finish my breakfast and head out. I am apprehensive.

"Captain's putting together a long-range patrol this morning," Ben states as if to inform me.

I nod, my mouth full of some salty dried meat that reminds me of my father's dried venison.

In a couple of days, the patrol will be leaving the green of the mountains and valleys and march into the Desert Sea. I am worried that it will be the first time into the Desert Sea for most of the soldiers.

Ben continues to stare out the window at the soldiers packing their gear. "I thought the company leaves for Salkhad in two days. Wonder where they're going?"

I glance out the window, knowing I am going with them. The sunlight has not broken over the wall yet, and the courtyard has a faint orange glow. I know we will be ready to leave soon. I have only the rucksack my father gave me, sitting by the table at my side. I look down; my whole life is in that bag: a small sketchbook with charcoal wrapped in paper, my grandfather's brass compass, a Bedouin robe given to me along with a small curved-blade dagger, and my mother's Bible. That reminds me ... I should grab more of this dried meat before I leave.

The lever-action Winchester rifle that my father gave me when I was thirteen to hunt white-tailed deer is leaning against the table. The gun is involved in the only fond memories I have of him. It is a Model 1894, like my father's; mine is the shorter version with the twenty-inch barrel. My father nicknamed my Winchester, "Spitz." Whenever we were on the hunt, my father referred to Spitz with pride; it is accurate and sharp, and shoots true.

Those hunts were the closest times my father and I shared. When I ran away from home, Spitz was the first thing I grabbed, along with my hunting pack, which was full of ammo. Spitz has never left my side; I have carried her across the Desert Sea. Luckily, I have never needed to use her and have kept her wrapped in oilcloth. This is the first time since I left home that she has been free of the protective covering.

I stand, grab my rucksack, and sling Spitz over my shoulder.

"Where are you going?" Ben asks.

I wish not to answer. I look toward the soldiers preparing for the long-range patrol.

"Wait, you're going with them? What ...?" Ben stutters.

I can see the question in his eyes: How could his friend go on this mission and not tell him, and especially *without* him?

He follows me to the kitchen, where I ask the cook for more dried meat.

10 [rucksack] - F.M. Jäger (c. 1917)

"Where are you going? I should probably go with you."

"The major wants me to go because I speak Arabic and he wants an interpreter with his patrol." The cook hands me the wrapped meat, and I quickly stuff it into my rucksack.

"Wait, why didn't you tell me?"

"I didn't know until late last night." It's a lame excuse; I quickly correct myself. "I wanted you to come, but I didn't know if it is proper to ask the captain."

Ben follows me into the courtyard.

"Look," I add, "I don't know any of this soldiering stuff. It was not like he asked me, more like an order. I didn't know if I should or even could ask if you could come, or even if you wanted to."

Ben is calm; he understands my dilemma.

The captain walks over and inspects the soldiers tying the gear onto the pack-camels. He looks over at me and nods, a signal that they are ready.

I turn to Ben. "I will see you soon."

"Mare! Steady on," he replies.

I give him a salute, and he snaps to attention, returning the salute as if giving me permission to carry on. It is an honest gesture, and it makes me feel like one of the men. I continue over to Captain Wilson and the patrol as they prepare to leave.

"Mr. Jäger," Captain Wilson says to me formally, "we've seen more activity of Arabs heading north in the past few months. This is a scouting mission to assess activity in the area as we make our advance to Mar Musa. Your destination is some old ruins about twelve days' ride north from here.

We believe the ruins may be a base of operations. Lieutenant Richards will be leading this long-range patrol to Masyaf; Lieutenant York and his patrol group will accompany to Mar Musa, fortify the position, and send word back to Fifth Company. If you run into any Bedouins, you're to assist Lieutenant Richards with any translations. If you find anything of interest, please take detailed notes." A look of concern washes over his face. "If there are any problems, you are to hold fast at Mar Musa and wait for Fifth Company."

It is an odd speech, and I quickly catch on: The captain has not shared with Lieutenant Richards our discussion from the previous evening.

"Yes, sir, I understand." I turn and nod to Lieutenant Richards to show him respect and that I am under his command.

Tuff is ready and packed. I get in the saddle and lean over to tell her, "Tuff, it's you and me now." She rises, prepared for our journey into the Desert Sea.

The captain approaches. I can tell he wishes to say something privately, and I lean over.

"Keep your head about you," he says. Then he pulls his pistol from his belt, and spins it to offer me the handle. I take it, stashing it in my belt.

The sun crests the wall, and for the first time, I look to the north. Soon, the Desert Sea will once again lie before me, along with the unknown.

* * *

The two patrols follow the wadi, and we reach the Rhube Oasis without incident two days from Salkhad. We are to top off on water at the oasis and prepare for crossing the Desert Sea. In the Desert Sea, we will find no water for four days, perhaps five.

This is the last oasis, the last place with water and trees. I am unsure if the men are ready for the crossing. The Desert Sea is not as forgiving as the Sinai.

Ben and Fifth Company should be arriving at Salkhad any day. If we make it safely to Mar Musa, we will send word and have Fifth Company's Lieutenant York's Rifle Section and Ben's Machine-gun Section follow in a week, followed by Lieutenant Richard's Section.

Lieutenant York is far more friendly than Lieutenant Richards, who is rather aloof and does not wish to hear from me, so I issue a reminder to the friendlier lieutenant. "Lieutenant York, we need to make sure to carry extra water. There is no place to stop for water for a few days if we wish to avoid the Turks."

"Thank you, Mr. Jäger, good advice, and I will see we have enough. Lieutenant Richards assures me it should take three days."

"Five," I say under my breath, but I know Lieutenant York hears me. He knows of my concern about Lieutenant Richards.

"We will make sure to carry enough water."

"We should rest by day and travel by night; it's cooler at night, and we can make better time." I urge.

"I'll share your suggestion with Lieutenant Richards," Lieutenant York says, though he knows it will be a wasted effort. Lieutenant Richards wishes not to hear suggestions from anyone. He likes to remind his men that he is of a respected bloodline of English lords who have proudly served the Crown for generations. Lieutenant Richards is perturbed someone else will be leading his Second Section to Mar Musa.

"Jones, you have the watch. Ready camp," Lieutenant Richards commands. He is all orders. Lieutenant Richards keeps his distance from the men. I have spoken with him only a few times, the conversations short, simple commands—mostly orders to help Smitty. "Mr. Jäger, assist Smitty," Lieutenant Richards says, reminding me that I am not without orders and am, as always, to assist the cook.

"Yes, sir."

"Ne'r mind thuh Lootenant, he's a cock robin. Spends all 'is time writ'n love notes to thuh misses." Smitty tells me. I have grown accustomed to his broken colonial Indian slang wrapped in a barely understandable Cockney accent. He is the friendly face among the men.

Smitty was born in India, the son of an Indian woman and a British soldier. He never knew his mother. His father returned to England with Smitty in tow and died a drunk. Smitty grew up in the seedier side of London, and when all else looked bleak, he joined the King's Army. Although he is mixed-race, part wog, his cooking and humor have won the men's hearts and friendship. I am fond of Smitty and his easy, jovial ways. Nothing seems to bother him, even this mission, which weighs heavily on the men. Smitty's jokes and hearty laugh always come at the right time. He has a second sense for tension and knows how to bring an ease to the men when they need it most. There is stress in the air as we prepare to make the long desert crossing, and Smitty is our salvation amidst the tension.

In stark contrast to Smitty is Jones. If there ever is one to find a problem with something, it is Jones. The heat, his ass sore in the saddle, the sand ... it is always something. By the time we arrive at the oasis, Smitty has had enough of Jones's complaining, saying the man is as useless and as annoying as a dilberry. It has stuck, and Jones's nickname among the men is Dilberry, to his irritation—but it has stopped his complaining. I know Jones is not ready for the desert crossing. I have a feeling he will not live to see Masyaf.

Of the five men other than Smitty in Lieutenant Richards's patrol group, I converse only with Sergeant Sauer. He is a quiet and intense fellow whom the other soldiers call Sergeant Sour behind his back, though they are careful as not to let him hear. They keep their distance, and even the lieutenant avoids engaging with him. Sergeant Sauer served in the German Army before the war. Although accepted by the English into the King's Army, he keeps a distance from his fellow soldiers because of his German accent. He is *boche*, after all, and the English are dying by the thousands on the Western Front. The Battle of the Somme took a heavy toll on the English.[26]

Much like Smitty for not being entirely British, Sauer is a reminder to the British of their enemy, yet the men have an unspoken respect for Sergeant Sauer. Perhaps it is fear, or maybe because he is the oldest and most experienced soldier among them. His frame and stature cause him to tower over the other men, and if anyone were to come upon our small patrol, they would assume him to be the leader.

"*Guten Abend, Herr* Sauer."

"*Guten Abend. Du sprichst Deutsch.*" Sergeant Sauer seems surprised.

"*Ja, mein Vater ist Deutscher, und ich habe als Kind Deutsch gelernt.*"

Sergeant Sauer is pleased to be speaking in his native tongue, and we exchange stories of family and home. I speak of my grandmother's German springerle cookies and learn that he, too, was fond of springerles as a boy.

The conversation ends as abruptly as it began. Sergeant Sauer stands, slings his rifle over his shoulder. Towering in frame, he looks down at me. In English, he says, "Nice to meet your acquaintance, *Herr* Jäger. You should get some rest; it is a long journey ahead, und I have zee watch."

He is focused on the mission. If there are to be problems, I want to be close to him—he seems the most capable of the lot.

I wash dinner down with the foul-tasting water from the oasis and head over to the mess to start cleaning the dishes, my routine assignment.

"Interpreter; more like a maid," I mumble to myself. I do not realize Sergeant Sauer is standing before me.

He hands me his plate and nods with respect. "Glad tha boche is serving thuh king," Smitty says, placing his hand on my shoulder and nodding toward Sergeant Sauer as the sergeant walks away.

"Sergeant Sauer is a good man."

" 'Tis well he is. Now grind thuh tins," Smitty retorts, ordering me to wash the plates.

I prefer to sleep outside and next to Tuff, my camel, as I have done in my travels with the Bedouin. The Bedouin know the camel is not just a beast of burden but also an intricate part of the desert. I was told the camels are the keepers of desert secrets; take care of them, and they will take care of you. Come to think of it, I much prefer the company of camels to the company of this lot of the king's soldiers. I fall asleep resting against my camel, my companion, feeling safe.

I never really mind a Desert Sea crossing; in fact, I look forward to it as a mental game—and one of solitude. The Desert Sea is the one place I can think. The Bedouin travel the Desert Sea in their own time, not too slow but never rushed. Theirs is a pace, a rhythm, set by the camels. The camels know how far they can travel and where there is water; they are as much a part of the desert as is the sand.

* * *

Eventually, on a Desert Sea crossing, you give way to the pace of the camel. After our third day in the long crossing, Lieutenant Richards finally takes my suggestion, and we begin traveling by night when it is cool. This helps, but the Desert Sea has already started draining the life from the men's souls. We need to find Mar Musa soon.

On the morning of the fifth day in the Desert Sea, Jones has fallen back. His complaining has stopped, and like the rest of the men, he has fallen silent. Even complaining requires a lot of a man under the sun's anvil. The vastness and emptiness hit them hard when they are not ready for the crossing.

You can prepare physically for a long desert crossing, but it is a mental game. I do my best to keep the men from drifting. The moment your mind wanders, you forget to drink, forget where you are, get lost, or—worse—fall from your camel to be consumed by the Desert Sea. I ride along, tapping them with a cane to wake them. If we come upon the enemy, they will not be ready. Only Lieutenant York and Sergeant Sauer seem fit for this; they have made crossings before, I can see.

Finally, I see the rock formation marking the hidden path leading into the mountains, to Mar Musa. The sky is red and orange; soon, the sun will be upon us. I ride up to Lieutenant Richards, who is drifting. I tap him with my cane, and he snaps out of it. I point the cane toward the mountain and turn. He turns to follow.

"Mr. Jäger?" His voice cracks. I know he drank all his water the day before.

I hand him my waterskin. "Two sips," I whisper.

He gulps it down; water pours down his face.

"It's there, the path to Mar Musa." I point again.

"Where?"

He would have marched right by the path; even most Bedouins cannot see it. The trail is hidden from the untrained eye. Mar Musa does not exist to most of the world, its name and location are known to only a few.

I reach over and grab my waterskin. "Not far. Follow."

I lead the men along the path, to what seems to be nowhere. Shortly, around a bend, appear the ruins of

Mar Musa in high elevation above the ravine. The final approach is carved in stone.

I feel as if time has stopped here. I was likely the last visitor, no one else here expect the two monks who live in the one old ruin.

11 Desert Sea - F.M. Jäger (c. 1917)

CHAPTER 6

Mar Musa

Mar Musa consists of several stone buildings, a tower, and a courtyard. Several rooms and structures have also been carved into the walls of the ravine. It is larger than I remember. The same two monks are here, apparently never having left. I greet them, and they nod cautiously, looking at the British soldiers. They keep to only one building, a chapel. The rest of Mar Musa has been untouched by man for hundreds, perhaps thousands, of years.

We are to stay only one night in Mar Musa, to the men's chagrin. The men are exhausted, but Lieutenant Richards wastes no time; we are to continue to Masyaf as ordered and to rendezvous back at Mar Musa. We spend the afternoon preparing the camels and loading provisions.

Lieutenant Richards hands over a satchel to Lieutenant York, "my notes and report for Captain Wilson are in here, see that he gets it." He pauses and pulls a letter from his shirt, "please make sure this is posted."

Lieutenant York's eyebrows raise with a smile. Lieutenant Richards is having none of it, turns and walks away.

"Probably another love letter to his wife," I mumble when Lieutenant Richard is out of earshot.

"Wife? He's not married," Lieutenant York turns to me with a look of surprise. "The letter is addressed to his sister."

"I just thought…"

Lieutenant York interrupts, "she's a nurse serving somewhere in Europe I hear. Best keep your thoughts to yourself." He pats me on the shoulder and hails to one of his men as he turns to leave.

Lieutenant York and his men survey Mar Musa. He will leave two men from his patrol to begin fortifications of Mar Musa. Lieutenant York and the rest of his patrol will leave in the morning, back across the Desert Sea to Salkhad. They have mapped our journey for Fifth Company's Rifle Section and Machine-gun Section to make the Desert Sea crossing, and I look forward to seeing Ben and Captain Wilson when they arrive.

The sun has set over the mountains, and the sky is a canvas of colors: orange, reds, and purples. I look forward to the rest before our journey to Masyaf. Unlike the soldiers who seek shelter among the ruins of Mar Musa, I sleep with Tuff, my camel. My sleep is uneasy. I have brought the British Army to the solitude of Mar Musa; it will never be the same again.

* * *

My eyes open slowly; Tuff is stirring just enough to tell me to wake quietly. Mar Musa is glowing in the blue light of the moon; all is quiet as the soldiers sleep away their aches and pains from their first desert crossing. Something is wrong.

My right hand instinctively grabs the handle of my curved Bedouin dagger below the blanket; a gun would be too loud. I slow my breath and listen. Then I roll over on my belly and shuffle quietly so as to surveil my surroundings. I see a cloaked figure creeping along the other side of the ravine. Scanning to my left, I see Jones sitting with his head down and rifle resting against his shoulder. Asleep! I shake my head. He is useless.

I scamper down and across the ravine to garner a closer look at the stranger or to make my way to safety. I move quickly and silently, my knife at the ready until I am several feet behind the cloaked onlooker. No rifle. Movement seems as if he is curious, not threatening. Clothes look Bedouin, but I cannot be sure.

I scan the horizon for any other potential intruders.

I call out in a whisper, "*Hal beemkani mosa'adatuk?*" *Can I help you?* The words come naturally.

The stranger turns slowly, and I begin to regret my encounter. I can see the outline of his face. My hand firmly grips to the dagger, ready to meet my end or his. He closes the distance between us quickly and silently.

The moon lights his face, and I recognize his smile.

"*Ahlan sadiqi! Eshtaqto elaika! Kaifa haloka?*" *My friend! I miss you! How are you?* he asks.

We embrace in the usual Bedouin manner, almost European, but with a sniff rather than a kiss to each check.

Hasan ibn Faraj is a Bedouin. His father, Faraj, is a king of one of the Bedouin tribes. Hasan, once a prince of a kingdom, is now a fighter and tracker. We became close friends—more like brothers—when I met him at a bazaar and joined his caravan several years ago, before the war. He was eager to improve his English, and he helped me learn Arabic. I embraced the customs and wore the traditional clothing of his people. I was not like the other English and was soon adopted by his family and lived with them.

"I am glad to see you too, brother. What are you doing in these parts, this far west?" I speak in English, which he prefers, as he loves to practice. Hasan's people are from the northeastern part of the Desert Sea. I have never known them to travel beyond it except during their pilgrimage to Mecca.

"Talk of Caecus at Salkhad," he replies.

I forgot that Bedouin spies and information travel like a silent river. The British could learn from them—if they did not disrespect the Bedouin so much.

"Please don't call me that; you know I hate it," I remind him. Caecus is a nickname I could do without, but it has stuck.

"Hasan came; Cae … Mare was gone," he stumbles, correcting himself. "Track English to Rhube Oasis. I knew you would come to Mar Musa. English smell and loud, can hear from Cairo," Hasan says with a smile. He has little respect for the English, even though they are allies in this war. It is lost on the British Army, blinded by arrogance and pride, that they leave a noticeable trail for anyone to follow.

12 Hasan 1917 - F.M. Jäger (c. 1917)

"You found me. Let's go back, and we can talk and have tea. I'll introduce you to Lieutenant Richards and Lieutenant York. They are good men."

His tone and mood change from friendly to somber. "No, Hasan is not here. *Ta'ala ma'ee!*" I am to follow him.

Seeing Hasan brings back great memories. We ventured together throughout the Desert Sea before the war. Over a short period of time I learned Arabic and the stories of the hidden histories and myths. I traveled with Hasan on the great pilgrimage to Mecca in 1914, just before the war began. I am probably the only white man other than Sir Richard Burton,—and indeed am the first American—to have traveled to Mecca.

I also remember the story of how I received the nickname, Caecus, which I would as soon forget.

* * *

Muqla was the keeper of the scrolls. He seemed very old but moved with grace. His eyes were blue, clouded, and he never made eye contact. He seemed blind but moved as if he had sight. His name was Sapiente, but I had given him the nickname Muqla Dakana, which loosely translates from Arabic as Eyeball Smoke. *My Arabic was horrible, and it was the best translation I could come up with for the English nickname, Smoky Eyes, I'd created for him.*

Hasan and his sister, Roxana, thought the nickname was funny. My attempt at a nickname was horrible, but the name Muqla sounded so odd that we all came to call him Muqla. One of us would say, "Mooo KLA," and we would just laugh and laugh. I had never seen Roxana laugh

13 Muqla Sapiente - F.M. Jäger (c. 1914)

so much. We never mentioned the name to his face; it was our personal and private joke.

One day, Hasan was ordered to attend his first military council, comprised of all the Bedouin tribes. War had broken out between the Ottoman and British Empires. It was an important day for Prince Hasan, for this was the first step to bring him into his father's inner circle.

"Collect yourself for your father," Muqla ordered, his eyes never making contact. As they turned to leave, Muqla stopped and turned back to me. "Adam cannot go without his Eve! The council will not wait." Hasan laughed; I was again the subject of Muqla's wit.

Muqla led us to the grand council chambers. The grand table was full, except for one chair next to the king. Hasan was no longer the young prince; he was about to take his place at the king's side. Perhaps one day, he would rule the most powerful Bedouin tribe in the Desert Sea.

"Stand with dignity and do not speak," said Muqla. He pushed me toward the wall with his staff, then grabbed Hasan's hand like he would a child and began walking him to his seat. "Your father will not wait. Join him now."

Halfway across the council chamber, Muqla came to a halt and whispered to Hasan. Hasan's face grew serious. Muqla let go of Hasan's hand, and Hasan took a seat next to his father. Muqla stood behind the king and the prince.

One of the members of the council gave a detailed report of the Ottoman Army, mainly consisting of Turks. The Turks, with the Germans, had moved south and were seeking the aid of Bedouins willing to fight for the Ottoman Empire. The Turks would be passing by in days.

The king did not say a word. He sat quietly thinking, then turned to me.

"Marion, you know of the English. The Turks oppress the Bedouin, but we are of Asil. This is not a war of our choosing, but I believe it will be our war. We do not like the Turks, but what of the English?" asked the king.

All eyes turned to me. The room fell silent, and I could hear my own heartbeat. My palms began to sweat, for what was I to say? I am an American; America and England were allies.

I felt the best decision was to leave so the king would not have to make a choice. I did not want to speak for the English or suggest to the king that he pick a side.

As I began to reply that we should probably leave before the Turks arrived, I noticed Muqla start to leave the council chamber.

"Sapiente, have you no interest in what Marion has to say?" the king asked him.

The old man stopped and faced the king's general direction without looking at anyone.

The room fell silent, and slowly, all turned to face Sapiente. When the place seemed the stillest it could possibly get, Sapiente said, "Mutus, surdus, caecus!" He turned and left with a purposeful stride.

I knew some Latin and recognized what he said as "Deaf, dumb, and blind." Hasan looked at me and shook his head; I knew he understood, too, and we would never hear the end of it from Muqla. The others at the council, not understanding what Muqla had said, looked at each other and shrugged.

The king began to laugh. He turned to me and said, "Sapiente means wise *in Latin, best we remember." There was a slight pause, and then he concluded, "Caecus."*

* * *

That was how the king gave me the nickname Caecus, the blind. I wondered if the king knew of my nickname for Sapiente. From that moment on, everyone called me Caecus, and perhaps it was a deserved nickname.

Now, I miss the king and Sapiente. I felt joy at being adopted by their family, and I remember their warmth ... and now it saddens me to remember. Their kingdom is scattered, and Hasan, once a proud and educated prince, is a nomad.

I follow Hasan, the moon lighting our way. Near where his camel is resting, he opens a pack and removes a small bundle. "Here, look!" he says, handing it to me.

I begin to unwrap the bundle. When I am almost finished, Hasan's hand rests upon mine, stopping me. He whispers a short prayer, releases my hand, then nods for me to continue.

In the center of the cloth is a dagger. Strange darkness, blacker than the darkest night, surrounds the blade. "Hasan? What is this?" I ask, my voice low.

"Saladin's *Hidayah*," he whispers as he stares directly into my eyes.

"King Faraj is with Allah ..." He pauses, then continues with the Bedouin proverb: "I and my brother are against my cousin; I and my cousin are against the stranger!" He quickly rewraps the dagger without looking at it, then presses the bundle to my chest.

Now I am even more confused. The king, his father, is dead? I stand, staring, in shock. The Bedouin proverb means trouble—trouble for all.

Hasan turns again to his camel's pack, from which he removes a leather-bound scroll. "*Aṣabīya!*" he says. It means "solidarity among all." His hands are shaking as he hands me the scroll.

"What does it say?"

"*Sharaf.* Mare ... *hamasa!*" Hasan's tone is severe and defensive as he invokes the sacred Bedouin code of honor to call on my bravery and courage. This means his life and mine are in danger.

I stuff the scroll into my shirt as the sky turns purple. The sun will rise soon. The night watch will be changing rapidly—perhaps Jones had an excellent nap—and Smitty will be getting dried meat and tea ready for breakfast. I must get back.

Hasan has already mounted his camel by the time I come to this realization.

"Hasan, what did Muqla whisper to you?" I ask.

Hasan smiles, remembering the day his father, the king, gave me the nickname Caecus. " 'Wisdom flows from the spring of knowledge and experience. Today you drink from the spring, but one drink does not make one wise.' " Hasan's voice is somber, and I hear Muqla in the words.

"*Ma'a salama,*" I say with a bow.

"Caecus, what will be, will be," he says, nodding, doing well to hide any look of concern.

I watch him ride over the ridge to the west, wondering if I will ever see him again.

Finally, I scamper across the bridge. Tuff's head raises slowly. She looks upon me approvingly, knowing I am safe and the desert is watching over me.

I will not speak to Lieutenant Richards of my encounter, but I wonder if I should mention it to Captain Wilson or Major Bassett.

I place the leather-bound scroll and bundled dagger in my rucksack, roll up my gear, and walk over to the mess area to enjoy one of Smitty's welcoming breakfasts.

"Oy, swaddy, skof and ta wet?" comes through Smitty's broken smile as he offers me some meat and tea.

"Could be the bother," I say with a nod. Smitty smiles; it pleases him that I attempt to speak his custom slang minus the Cockney accent.

I take the plate of dried meat and a cup of tea up a small trail about the ruins to watch the sunrise. We will soon be traveling to Masyaf.

CHAPTER 7

An Enfield's Song

After only a day's rest in Mar Musa, we travel north three days through the Desert Sea toward Masyaf. It is day fourteen, two weeks since we left Azraq. Our long-range patrol appears battle-scarred—not by bullets or bombs but by Mother Nature. Her relentless sun and blasting sand have given Lieutenant Richards's patrol a pounding.

Dilberry and another of the men, Reynolds, are shells of the men they were at the start of this journey; I am surprised they have made it this far. Smitty is tired but never complains. Only Sergeant Sauer continues unwaveringly.

If we run into trouble, I have little faith in Lieutenant Richards. I will stay close to Sergeant Sauer; nothing seems to faze him.

When we finally reach the edge of the Desert Sea, I pull the scarf from my face to take a deep breath and stare across the horizon. With a slight smile, I close my eyes slowly; I do not want it to be a mirage. I reopen my eyes, hopefully, to see the ruins of Shmemis. We've made it!

Shmemis, the ruins of an ancient castle on a small mountaintop has marked civilization for more than two thousand years, a lighthouse on the edge of the Desert Sea. Bedouin caravans search for it after a desert crossing. Once, after a long journey in which man and beast had perished, I saw a Bedouin fall to the ground, praying to Allah, at the sight of Shmemis. It is a sign of life.

Soon, we will be in the green foothills giving rise to the Alawiyin Mountains. Masyaf lies only a day's ride away, on a high plateau at the mountain's steeps. I have seen the ruins of Masyaf only from a distance, as the Bedouins avoid the shadows of Masyaf, believing the place is cursed.

"Lieutenant, there ... Masyaf!" Jones's voice is raspy from the dry desert air. It has been unstable and cracking since the day we left the Rhube Oasis nearly nine days ago.

Lieutenant Richards, doing his best to hide his own physical exhaustion, ignores Jones and rides on. I follow the lieutenant, whispering to Dilberry Jones as I pass, "That is Shmemis. Masyaf is another day's ride."

We approach the hill on which rest the ruins of Shmemis, our camels trudging in a switchback fashion to the plateau. A small gully, like a mote, surrounds the crumbling walls. A gentle cool breeze kicks up a little sand, and we see the green of the mountains in the distance.

"Mr. Jäger!" Lieutenant Richards calls, and his vigor returning as he beckons me forth.

"Yes, sir?"

"How far to Masyaf?" he asks, looking at his map and compass. I wonder if he even knows how to use them; I was the one who led the patrol from Azraq to Salkhad, on to the Rhube Oasis, across the Desert Sea to find the

14 Shmemis A sing [sign] of life - F.M. Jäger (c. 1917)

hidden trail to Mar Musa, and now to Shmemis. Tomorrow, I will also be leading the men to the ruins of Masyaf.

I reach into my pocket, my fingers touching the warmth of my reliable brass compass, once my grandfather's. The old compass has saved my life more times than I care to remember, though the Bedouin do not use a compass, as navigation is in their blood. They showed me how to read the zenith of the sun and the traverse of the moon and stars—skills I cannot live without.

I point west toward Masyaf. "It's about forty miles. We can make it in a day if we leave at first light." I look back, to where Jones and Reynolds sit lazily on the ground. "The men need rest."

Lieutenant Richards raises his binoculars, searching the horizon. "We will camp here. This place?" he asks, never making eye contact.

"Shmemis. I have been here before. A landmark used by the Bedouins when crossing the desert. I would not have a fire," I suggest. "It can be seen for miles." Our camp on top of a mountain would not be hidden, and a fire would alert anyone nearby to our presence, though most likely, the enemy knew the moment we crossed the Desert Sea. Between our noise, tracks, and smell, every Arab from Damascus to Aleppo likely knows we are here. I can only hope they do not know of Mar Musa.

"Right … that will be all," he says, dismissing me as he continues to search the horizon.

I walk down to the gully below the walls. Only Sergeant Sauer is standing; the rest of the patrol sit with dreary heads, hoping we will break for camp. The Desert Sea has taken its toll.

Lieutenant Richards arrives moments later, keen to make his own entrance as if it matters. "We will make camp within the walls at the top. Double the watch standing this evening. Jones, Reynolds, you are the first watch. Smitty, a strong set of rations. No fires." He pauses, knowing he is forgetting something, then adds, "Mr. Jäger, fill the canteens."

The lieutenant marches off to surveil the surroundings, map and compass in hand, all for the show, perhaps to give his men comfort that he can glean insight from the tools of his trade. I postulate that he walks blindly through the routine exercises to mask his fear of the unknown.

A double watch with only four men. Surely, Lieutenant Richards will not stand watch, and I doubt he will place trust in me. The men will be lucky to have a solid four hours of sleep between each watch. Lieutenant Richards's orders, driven by fear of the unknown, will drain the men of needed rest. If we are to face battle, three well-rested men are better than four tired souls.

The men mumble discontent as Lieutenant Richards takes on the role of Captain Bligh. I wonder who will play the part of Fletcher Christian?[27]

"*Herr* Jäger, stay close to camp und do not wander off tonight." Sergeant Sauer stands beside me, staring toward the Desert Sea. Sergeant Sauer is not on the first watch, but I suspect he will be alert and at the ready. Does he know of my night meeting with Hasan?

"No fire dis night. Meats and nocks for the men," Smitty calls to me.

No fire means no hot meals. *Nocks* is Smitty's word for what passes as a biscuit ... the hardest, driest biscuit

you've ever seen. Hard enough to slay Goliath. The meat
is smoked venison, dried. Heavily salted, without water,
it can cause one to choke.

The tired men nod to me as I hand out Smitty's dinner of dried meat and rock-hard biscuit. I collect their
canteens to fill from the extra waterskins we carry.

"*Bleibe wachsam. Wir sind nicht alleine,*" whispers Sergeant Sauer as I hand him his filled canteen. *Stay alert, we
are not alone.* I stare at him, and he looks away, taking a
drink from his canteen. He knows we are in danger.

I walk down to the gully below the walls where the
camels are resting, wanting to be with Tuff if things go
wrong. I have little faith in Lieutenant Richards and the
men. I have learned that the open desert is a far better
place to be than trapped in some old ruins. Easier to see,
more comfortable to ride.

The soldiers set up on the hilltop, within the ruin
walls. They feel comfort behind walls, even if the walls
are in ruins. Walls and castles are in the English blood.

I notice Sergeant Sauer head toward the far side of the
gully, away from camp. It offers a better place from which
to watch for the enemy and a route to escape if needed.

All is quiet; the stars come out. I fall asleep hoping to
see tomorrow.

* * *

Tuff nudges me with force. I wake to see several figures
moving quickly and silently in across the camp in the
moonlight. Death is upon us; I can feel it.

A flash of lightning and a crack of thunder interrupt
their silent approach.

A moment later, I realize it is not thunder. It is Sergeant Sauer's Enfield erupting with death. The high-powered round catches a cloaked figure in mid-stride, dropping him like a heavy sack of potatoes. In a blink of the eye, another round is sent downrange. Another intruder drops. This time, a cloaked enemy makes a mistake, turning toward the sound of the Enfield, only to be met with another round. It catches him dead center, hurling him backward. Three bullets, three bodies.

I turn to see Sergeant Sauer focused, kneeling. He bolts in another round faster than seemingly possible. I have heard stories of expert marksmen accurately firing thirty shots at 300 yards under a minute but did not believe them until now, seeing how fast Sergeant Sauer is chambering and firing rounds. The Enfield is a cannon, firing a large .303 round.

"*Reiten!* RIDE!" Sergeant Sauer yells at me.

The fire of his gun has awakened the rest of the men, but too late. They are not prepared. They wake from dream-filled slumber to be met by the cloaked grim reaper; their minds not sufficiently alert to what is upon us all: death. They shuffle, tired from the little sleep of their burdensome double watch, trying to gain their balance and grab weapons.

I instinctively grab my knife and the commander's pistol and brandish them both for a fight. Sergeant Sauer rises, charging toward the enemy. Without thinking, I rush behind him, surprised by my own action.

In my adrenaline-fueled run, I trip, falling over. I stand, looking down to see what fouled my gait. Dilberry Jones's headless body. *How do I know it is Jones?* I am too puzzled by the horrifically unnatural sight to feel any-thing. My mind is only able to cobble together a rec-ognition of Jones's ill-fitting, stained uniform. *Where is Reynolds? He should have been standing watch!*

Sergeant Sauer raises his Enfield and fires again. The bullet plows through the back of a cloaked head, blasting out the face of a man. Blood splatters on the tent, and I watch a piece of pulpy flesh briefly stick to the tent's canvas. Sergeant Sauer slams the bayonet of his rifle into the back of another cloaked enemy and fires point-blank, blasting the enemy off of his bayonet skewer.

I follow behind Sergeant Sauer's trail of blood and horror, feeling safe despite the carnage. Memories of making sausage with my father, using his meat grinder, flash in my mind. Now Sergeant Sauer is the meat grinder.

Two enemies come charging. "*Hinter ihnen!*" erupts from my throat. Sergeant Sauer spins the butt of his Enfield with brutal force, causing a cracking sound as the gun catches the enemy's jaw, disfiguring his face, sending him to the deepest sleep, if not death.

Sergeant Sauer slashes to his left flank. The Enfield's bayonet slices the second enemy's stomach. The slice opens wide as the bloody innards pour from the gaping stomach mouth. In stunned disbelief, the enemy gazes down, his scrambling hands attempting to stuff the bloody entrails back into place. He fails to realize he is witnessing his own gruesome death.

Sergeant Sauer turns toward me, his stare reminding me of Father. I am in trouble, have disobeyed him, and perhaps disappointed him most profoundly.

"*Laufen!*" he bellows. I can see the terror in his eyes—not at what lies before us, but perhaps at what might befall me.

Reynolds is fighting off an enemy. I rush to his aid, but too late. A long dagger plunges deep into his stomach. He tries to cry out, but his scream is silent. I can see the life slip from his body as he falls forward against the enemy, who quickly pushes the lifeless body off in the most disinterested manner as if it is only a nuisance.

Lieutenant Richards is the only other of our men on his feet, his sword at the ready. He fires his pistol at the enemy. I am not sure if he manages to land a shot. He charges toward an enemy who stands over a dead British soldier, Smitty. The lieutenant screams with rage, swinging with such brutal force that his sword is buried deep into the bone of the enemy hovering over Smitty's body.

Another enemy rushes toward the lieutenant from behind, and I begin to yell out, but too late. The curved blade of the enemy strikes hard, decapitating the lieutenant. His headless body buckles and falls.

It is over; they are all dead.

From behind me, a hand snares my collar, yanking me hard to the ground. I am dragged across the hardpack, stunned, hearing cracks of pistol fire above me. Sergeant Sauer, covered in blood, fires his pistol, keeping the enemy at bay as he drags me from battle.

He lifts me with one hand and drops me on Tuff, who rises, ready to retreat.

"*Reiten!*" his voice echoes over the gunfire.

Sergeant Sauer turns and cracks an enemy's skull with his pistol, then pulls his trench knife, burying it in the enemy's throat. I stare as blood splurges from the enemy's mouth. Sergeant Sauer yanks the knife free and flings the blade toward another charging enemy. *Swish, thud,* the blade penetrates, dropping the enemy in mid-stride.

Tuff is eager to move, but she has a mind to wait for Sergeant Sauer.

He retrieves his trench knife from the body and mounts his camel. "*Reiten.* NOW!"

We ride hard and do not look back.

15 Attack on Shmemis - F.M. Jäger (c. 1917)

CHAPTER 8

Faraj's Duty

"*Aufwachen.* Wake Up." A hand is shaking me.

I am asleep, resting against Tuff. The tree we are under offers little shade from the late afternoon sun.

"Drink. Sun vill set soon. We vill ride at night, rest by day. We make Mar Musa in two days, no three days." Sergeant Sauer scans the horizon.

"Where ... where are we?" I have trouble forming words. My body wants to rest, and my head is in pain.

"Furqlus!" He points toward a small town a few hundred yards west.

"There may be water!" I believe it abandoned, knowing that nomads raided it before the war. At least there is shelter.

Sergeant Sauer shakes his head. "Zee Turks have a small garrison there now."

Suddenly, I remember the attack. I look north, back toward Shmemis. Sergeant Sauer puts his hand on my shoulder. "They are not following us. I have kept watch. We are safe," he says, looking toward Furqlus, "for now."

"You are ..." I point to his shirt. It is stained with dried blood.

"I vill be fine. Have some water, not too much; we have a long ride. Get some rest." He seems to be ignoring the pain, but I can see it on his face. He lies down next to his camel.

* * *

The sun begins to set, the sky turns orange, and the breeze starts to cool. We will ride south soon, traveling slowly. We will reach Mar Musa in three days if we make a reasonable distance in our condition. We barely escaped and have little food and water. I fear Sergeant Sauer's injuries are far worse than he lets on; he grows weak. I hope Captain Wilson and the rest of Fifth Company have reached Mar Musa.

"What were you doing zee other night?" Sergeant Sauer speaks in a quiet whisper. I thought he was resting.

"What?"

"Zee other night, at Mar Musa. I saw you sneak away. There vas someone else, a Bedouin." Sergeant Sauer is tired, but I can tell he has been burdened by this question for some time.

I explained about meeting Hasan, and the dagger.

"Let me zee zis dagger." He can barely muster the words.

I reach into my bag, unwrap the dagger, and hand it to him. It is the first time I have seen it in daylight. The pommel has a blue stone, which seems to glow when the sun hits it just right. The handle is white, and the blade, a smoky grey. I swear I see smoke swirling around the blade's edge briefly as I unwrap it.

Sergeant Sauer holds the dagger carefully and studies it closely. "Saladin's Hidayah ... Never knew ..." Sergeant Sauer's words trail off.

"What? How do you know?"

He looks over toward me and nods. "I vas in Africa for some years. I vas ordered to Libya before zee Tripoli War broke out.[28] Supposed to observe, but after zee Italians butchered women and children in Mechiya,[29] I joined zee Arabs und Turks to kill as many Italians as I could. I vas wounded at zee Battle of Tobruk."[30]

A faint smirk touches his face. "Italians are zee worst soldiers; they should stick to food and wine." There is a pause as he thinks of a time from long before. "They left me for dead after zee battle. A nomad found me; he vas with a small caravan traveling to Syria. I traveled with him, und he helped me recover. He called me Ortis."

"Ortis? Latin for 'origin'?"

He nods. "Yes. I stayed in Syria, a year until I vas well to travel. I learned Arabic und zee myths of Saladin, Sinān, und stories of zee Desert Sea. When I regained my strength, I return to zee Fatherland but vas captured and sent to England."

His story puzzles me. "Why join the King's Army?" I ask.

"Zee English knew I spent time in zee region und spoke Arabic. I vas to accompany an English archeological expedition to Syria. Zee mission vas a failure, und zee war broke out."

"Archeological expedition?"

"I vas not told much. I spoke Arabic und German. I vas there to be a soldier und interpreter. They kept zee mission secret; I did not know where we travel." He shook his head ever so slightly. "I vas to follow orders. I overheard them speaking of Saladin, battles of zee Crusades"—he looks down at the dagger—"und mention of Saladin's Hidayah. They had no idea I too learned of zee myths. I kept quiet und listened. I did what I vas told."

Sergeant Sauer looks up at the sky as it turns from orange to red in the setting sun. He is tired and weak but is still doing his best to hide it. "Our expedition vas attacked at night, like our long-range patrol at Shmemis. They killed everyone, left me for dead."

"Bad habit, being left for dead," I say with a slight smile.

He nods and leans over to hand me the dagger. As I reach for it, he grabs my arm firmly. "Who else knows?"

For the first time, I am scared of Sergeant Sauer. "No one. I did not say anything to anyone. You're the first. I swear."

He lets go. "Keep it that way. That is Saladin's Hidayah you have, und zee enemy knew, they would be upon us. Now get some rest; we leave in un hour. It is a long ride," he reminds me.

I turn to lie down, then pull the blanket from the saddle. It is getting cold. My backpack falls forward, and the leather-bound scroll Hasan gave me rolls out.

I unroll the scroll and begin to read the Arabic writing in the light of the setting sun a story of men and battles from long ago.

* * *

Saladin's Hidayah

Sinān learned of the Templars' search for a secret, which can turn men into gods. Sinān secretly met with Saladin and told him Masyaf must never fall to the Templars. Sinān would help Saladin defeat the Templars. Sinān gave Saladin a dagger, which would protect Saladin and provide him with guidance.

I and my brother are against my cousin; I and my cousin are against the stranger.

The Templars built a fort and temple at Zir'in,[31] which means the seed of God, in the Jezreel Valley in their quest for the secret. Saladin laid siege to the Templars' fort in the Battle of Al-Fule.[32] His army could defeat the Templars, but Saladin ordered his generals to retreat. He ordered his private guards to dress as religious pilgrims and ordered his soldiers to escort the "religious pilgrims" far into the Desert Sea to the east.

The Templars believed that they had defeated Saladin and that the religious pilgrims were protecting the secret they searched for. The Templars followed Saladin's religious pilgrims into the Desert Sea, never to be seen again. The Templars never learned of Masyaf, or what happened to the religious pilgrims who traveled into the desert. Saladin's defeat is one of his most notable victories.

Saladin returned to the deserted Templar castle in Zir'in and hid the dagger in the castle. Saladin told his most trusted advisors that Masyaf must never fall. He ordered them to protect the dagger and Masyaf against any enemy.

Long after Saladin's death, Kahn learned of this secret and the myth of Saladin's Hidayah, and the Mongols invaded Syria searching for the Hidayah.[33] The Kahn learned of Saladin's battle with the Templars in the Jezreel Valley. He ordered the Mongol commander, Kitbuqa,[34] to search the Jezreel Valley for Saladin's Hidayah.

Qutuz, the sultan of Egypt,[35] ordered his army to defend against the Mongol invasion. The sultan needed help and called on Baibars,[36] the commander of a small army of the Ayyubid,[37] once the great dynasty of Saladin. Baibars, like the commanders of Saladin before him, had secret orders to protect Masyaf and Saladin's Hidayah. Baibars agreed to help the sultan defeat the Mongols.

Baibars led his small army to meet the Mongols in the Jezreel Valley in the Battle of Ain Jalut.[38] He attacked the Mongols, but the sultan of Egypt ordered his own army to wait. The sultan watched the battle from safety, protected by his men. He tricked Baibars to fight for him.

When the sultan saw Baibars would be victorious, he ordered his army to join in the attack. It was too late; Baibars killed the Kahn's commander, Kitbuqa, in battle, and the Mongol army retreated before the sultan arrived.

Kahn never found Saladin's Hidayah, or Masyaf.

Word of Baibars's victory spread across the land. The sultan, humiliated, died a mysterious death. Baibars became the next sultan of Egypt and led his army to defeat the last of the Crusaders.

On Baibars's death, his most trusted friend and advisor, Faraj, returned Saladin's Hidayah to Zir'in. Faraj lived a long life with his wife. They had many sons, his sons had sons, and they had sons. For many years, the sons of Faraj protected Saladin's Hidayah and the secret of Masyaf, waiting for the day when the spirit of Sinān would visit and ask another to serve, to protect Masyaf.

* * *

Faraj? Prince Hasan Faraj? King Faraj. The dagger has been in their care since the days of the Crusades.

Why would he give it to me? Why would the English be looking for it? Is Sergeant Sauer right; are these cloaked enemies searching for it?

The myth is wrong. Sinān gave Saladin the dagger to protect Masyaf and defeat the Crusaders, not to threaten Saladin.

A wisp of smoke curls about the dagger, and the blue stone glows slightly. The sun has set, and I lean against my camel, resting, peering at the dagger. The moon reflects from the blade. What powers does the dagger hold, can this be a key to Masyaf?

16 Saladin's Hidaya - F.M. Jäger (c. 1917)

ACT 3:
A BEDOUIN'S
WARNING

CHAPTER 9

A Tuff Ride

Our progress is slow. With no food, little water, and Sergeant Sauer's injuries, the journey has taken longer than I expected. It has been three days since the attack at the ruins of Shmemis, and we had hoped to reach Mar Musa by now. In our hasty escape, we had no time to grab provisions, riding only with what we had, so we have been two days without food. The waterskin has enough to last us the day. We avoid villages on our way back; any friendly Bedouin tribes have moved south or joined the Arab Revolt. Between Turks and nomad scavengers, the villages are not safe, and I worry about lacking the strength to defend ourselves.

We arrive just north of Huwwarin, in the old ruins. Dawn is upon us, soon the sun will be beating down. It is time to rest, and ruins offer some shelter. Sergeant Sauer is very weak. I lift his head, and he sips from the last of our water. There is a well in the village, but I fear it is not safe. Bedouins are protective of the desert's lifeblood, water. I will preserve what we have; it is to be a long ride at night to Mar Musa.

Sergeant Sauer is barely conscious, too weak to ride. He is resting behind the walls of the ruins, avoiding the sun's heat. He is unable to ride; he will fall off. The only way to get him back is to make a stretcher. I work in the shade to find some branches and forge a stretcher from the saddle blanket. I lash it together with leather straps and torn cloth, which I twist into rope. I hope it will hold on our night's journey; Tuff will have to pull it.

Tuff seems to know what I am doing as I attach the stretcher to her. She nods slightly as if in approval; she too likes Sergeant Sauer. I am exhausted, my throat dry, and stomach aching with hunger. It will be up to Tuff to get us to Mar Musa; I can only promise myself that I will hang on. I need to rest now; I drink a sip from the water-skin. There is little left. I need to conserve my strength and rest. I lie in the shadows of the ruins and look over toward Sergeant Sauer. I watch for a long time to see if he still breathes. I pray he makes it.

* * *

I feel a nudge. It is Tuff waking me. The sky is dark; it is time.

I crawl over to Sergeant Sauer. I hear him breathing, which brings me hope. I grab the waterskin and lift Ser-geant Sauer's head. "Just one sip," I tell him. "We do not have much left. Mar Musa is close; please hold on." I speak softly, and I am not sure if he hears me. I pour just a little water in his mouth, unsure if he can swallow.

A slight nod of his head indicates it is enough.

It takes all my might to drag Sergeant Sauer onto the makeshift stretcher. Once I pull him onto it, he lifts his hand slowly and rests it on my arm; he knows I am doing the best I can.

Tuff kneels, but I can barely get on the saddle. I lean over to tell her, "Tuff, please get us home safely. Mar Musa."

* * *

I do not know how long we have been riding. My mind tells me I am drifting. I know I am, but there is nothing I can do. I can barely lift my head to see the horizon. The sun is starting to rise; the sky is a beautiful royal purple.

Church bells ring in the distance. I sway in the saddle, my mind drifting, a dream.

"Wounded!" echoes loudly in my ears.

Mar Musa. It must be.

Tuff kneels as soon as we enter the courtyard. She has pulled Sergeant Sauer all night, up the mountain pass. Tuff has saved our lives.

"Mare! Mare, it's me, Ben!"

I can barely make out Ben's face; it is a haze. But Ben's voice gives me comfort. It is not a dream; we truly made it.

Captain Wilson's voice barks orders. "Lieutenant York, grab some men and help Sergeant Sauer and Mr. Jäger to the hospital. Lieutenant Wright, go with them; make sure they are well taken care of."

* * *

I do not know how long I have slept. I awake to Ben sitting by my bed, his head down. I reach over and rest my hand on his shoulder.

He looks up and grins, that grin that only Ben has. It comforts me.

The door opens, and Captain Wilson walks in. "How are we feeling this morning?"

I smile and nod, not wishing to talk, as my throat hurts.

"Lieutenant Richards and the long-range patrol?" the captain asks, his face showing his concern.

I close my eyes slowly and shake my head.

"I see. Is there anything you can tell me?"

I try to speak, but it is difficult with my throat so dry. "All dead. At Shmemis. We never made it to Masyaf." I swallow painfully and continue, "Lieutenant Richards tried to hold them off. Too many of them." I cannot tell the captain that Lieutenant Richards failed and that Sergeant Sauer, whom few trust, is the real hero.

The captain places his hand on my arm as he asks, "Turks?"

"Nomad scavengers ... Fifteen, maybe twenty ... swords and knives ... no guns." My throat is beginning to hurt.

"Was it an ambush?"

"No ... at camp ... the lieutenant ..." I can no longer speak.

The captain pours some water from the pitcher and helps me hold the glass in my hands as I drink. "When

17 Tuff saving us after Shmemis - F.M. Jäger (c. 1917)

you are well enough, report to my quarters. I want a proper report. I need a full report from Sergeant Sauer when he wakes."

I stop drinking, "How's the sergeant?"

"He's still unconscious. Dehydrated, and a loss of blood said the doctor—" Ben interjects.

"That's enough, Lieutenant," the captain says harshly. "I believe you have some duties to perform?"

"Yes, sir." Ben stands and, remembering he is an officer in the King's Army, snaps to attention, salutes, and marches out of the room—of course, not without giving a quick turn, a smile, and wave to me.

I smile back.

"Mr. Jäger, the lieutenant is a fine young man, but I think there's more to this story, and I wish for you to keep it to yourself until we can speak further. The major has come to Mar Musa. He wishes to speak with you when you are well." The captain places the glass on the table. He walks out of the room, then stops just outside the door, turns, and gives me a quick salute. The salute is worth more to me than any thank-you.

***

I feel much better when I wake after a long sleep. My throat is still dry, but far better. I walk to Sergeant Sauer's room; I wish to speak with him. He is the only one I trust, and I am afraid we will not see the last of this cloaked enemy.

"Sergeant, I am glad to see you're well."

"Thank you, *Herr* Jäger; thank you for getting us back."

"It was Tuff; she got us back."

Sergeant Sauer smiles slightly and nods.

"I haven't told them anything about the dag—"

Sauer reaches over and grabs my wrist. "Not a word!" His voice cracks as the strength of his grip fades.

"I spoke to the captain, only about the attack and our escape. I tried to tell him it's Lieutenant Richards, who led the attack and ordered the retreat; I don't think he believes me."

Sergeant Sauer nods; his dry throat whispers, "I like zee captain, und zee major is no fool. I knew why zee major sent me. Lieutenant Richards had no experience on zee battlefield."

"Can I trust him?" I asked, referring to the captain.

"It is not about trust; it is about what one does with zee knowledge you share with them." He looks toward the door to make sure we are alone before speaking again. "I trust zee major and even zee captain, but I do not trust those he puts trust in. He vill no doubt tell his superiors everything, it is his duty." He closes his eyes briefly, and a calm look comes over him. "He is a career officer, a good man, those he serves are never to be trusted. Speak to him with respect, but remember what you tell him, you tell his superiors. I think you understand." He pats my hand. It is enough; he needs to rest.

I nod and promise myself to check on him in the afternoon.

* * *

The command quarters are set up on the second floor of the tower. I climb the stairs and enter.

"Mr. Jäger, it's nice to see you walking about." It is the first cordial greeting I have received from the enlisted man who serves as an aide.

"Thank you."

"The captain's expecting you."

Once I'm in the captain's office, he tells me, "Shut the door and please have a seat. I normally would not offer such a young man a strong drink, but with all the action you have seen …" The captain pours a drink into a cloudy glass and hands it to me.

Is this how officers converse, or is he trying to get me at ease?

Major Basset turns from the window where he has been standing, and he smiles at me.

"Thank you." I take a sip and cough.

The captain looks away, perhaps to hide his amusement. "Please tell me what happened, do not leave anything out," he says a moment later.

"It was Sergeant Sauer who fought them off and was first alerted to the attack."

Captain Wilson is writing hastily in a notebook lying in front of him. "Stop. Please start at the beginning. Is there anything you remember before that night?"

"Nothing. Every night was the same: Lieutenant Richards set the watch, we ate, we slept, we rode. Nothing happened until the evening."

"You didn't see anyone, no one before the attack?" inquires the captain.

I feel like he knows what happened, but there is no way. Only Sergeant Sauer knows I met with my friend.

"No one. We didn't see any Bedouin patrols, no Turks, not even a nomad or pilgrim. This area is not well traveled; the Bedouin say it is cursed."

Captain Wilson nods. "Go on."

"We arrived at the ruins of Shmemis."

"Shmemis?"

"Yes, it's an old ruined castle on a hill. The Bedouin use it as a lighthouse after crossing the desert. It is a day's ride to Masyaf. Lieutenant Richards broke for camp in the ruins and set a double watch. We had no fire at night. I decided to sleep with the camels, away from camp. Sergeant Sauer also slept away from camp as an extra lookout." My voice grows excited. "If it were not for Sergeant Sauer, we'd be dead!"

"You're probably right," the captain says soothingly, seeing that my nerves are rattled. "Did the watch sound the alarm?"

"No. Jones was killed first and quietly. I woke when Sergeant Sauer fired his gun. I saw Lieutenant Richards attack one with his sword before ..." Memories of the lieutenant's decapitation flood my mind, but I continue, "The other men never had time; it was too late. Sergeant Sauer tried to get to the lieutenant, but... Sergeant Sauer pulled me from battle, and we rode off as fast as we could."

The Captain is excited. "Who were they? You say they're not Bedouin or Turks, but can you be sure?"

"They're dressed in black, their faces covered, like nomad scavengers, thieves, murderers. I saw them once before when I traveled with a Bedouin caravan; they attacked a small group of pilgrims when we came upon them, but they fled. The scavengers are thieves, stealing and killing. They've been known to raid small villages." I shake my head thinking of them, "they are vultures; after a battle, they'll steal from the dead. They have no honor; they're outcasts."

"You think they just happened upon you and attacked? Have you ever heard of them attacking soldiers before?" The captain grew concerned; he seemed to already be aware of these nomads.

"Never. Even after Sergeant Sauer shot three of them, they continued to attack. A nomad scavenger would sooner run away than face guns. They fear soldiers." I am truly puzzled.

Major Bassett had returned to looking out the window as I told my story. Without turning, he began to speak. "Sergeant Sauer was attacked in a similar fashion once before, left for dead. It is one of the reasons I requested him to join the Second Battalion."

I had not known the major knew about Sergeant Sauer's attack.

The captain looks up at me from his notebook. "Do you believe there could be more? Could this Masyaf be their fort?" He pauses, then adds in a hushed voice, "Are they Assassins?"

The thought did not occur to me until he uttered the word.

"Sir, I did not see any camps. I'm not a soldier or expert in these matters. I have never seen an Assassin."

"Right, but I do value your opinion. You are the only one to survive, save Sergeant Sauer. Your eyes are a witness, and I must listen to file the report and determine the next course of action," Captain Wilson tells me as he resumes writing in his notebook.

"Action?" I erupt.

"We are to prepare for an assault. If this enemy is bold enough to attack the British Army, they may be bold enough to attack us at Mar Musa," states the major as he turns from the window.

"I have already doubled the watch," the captain tells Major Bassett. "We will need to hold off any action as our main forces move north. We will be prepared for anything the enemy has in store for us."

"What of the Fifth Company?" I question.

The major looks at the captain and then to me.

"Fifth Company's Second Section was attacked on its way here," says the captain with a somber look.

"In the Desert Sea?"

"Damn!" The captain is upset. "No, not in the Desert Sea."

The major steps toward Captain Wilson, saying, "It's not your fault."

"What … what happened?" I ask uncertainly.

Major Bassett turns to me, as Captain Wilson is at a loss for words. "We have the rifle section and Second Lieutenant Wright's machine-gun section. That will have to be enough for now." The major turns back to Captain Wilson, "Fifth Company's reinforcements should arrive soon."

"Yes, sir!" The captain stands and leaves the room.

"Mr. Jäger, we're glad you're here. Now get some rest."

CHAPTER 10

Art of the Blade

A couple of days after my report to Major Bassett and Captain Wilson, I am feeling better, and Ben is eager to hear everything, hungry for a story about the action. "Join me for morning rations. You must share; I want all the details!"

"Ben, what happened?" I asked, to shift his attention. "The major said there are only a rifle section and your machine-gun section of the Fifth Company here."

Ben shook his head. "Captain Wilson led both Lieutenant York's and my section to Mar Musa. The Lieutenant Richards' Second Section was to arrive a couple of days after."

"What happened?"

"Second Section is commanded by a new captain, one of General Townshend's officers. He decided to avoid the desert and head north, just south of Damascus. They ran into a Turkish garrison. I am not sure how many we lost. They retreated back to Salkhad."

"I am sorry."

Ben nods, and I can tell he does not wish to speak of it. He has some friends who may have fallen.

As we enter the mess hall, Ben's mood improves, and he is still keen on hearing the story of what happened to me and Sergeant Sauer. "Tell me what happened?"

"There's not much to tell, it happened so fast," I say as we sit at a table.

"Come now, there must be something," he says.

I feel a slap on the back. It's Lieutenant York, who says, "Mr. Jäger, glad to see you about. Yes, please share the tale." He sits, joining us for breakfast. Two others join, and it is the first time I feel accepted by the officers.

"We made camp at some ruins a day's ride from Masyaf. Lieutenant Richards ordered a double watch and knew we'd entered enemy territory. We did not have a fire at night—"

"Yes, sounds like Lieutenant Richards, prepared for the enemy. Always keep an eye on those wogs!" one of the officers chimes in.

Lieutenant York waves his hand. "Let Jäger finish now."

"I woke when I heard shots fired. Sergeant Sauer was firing into the enemy as they entered the camp. I grabbed the pistol—"

Sergeant Sauer interrupts as he sits next to me. "It vas Lieutenant Richards's shots Jäger heard. He fired first, killing three. Jones und Reynolds were engaged in hand-to-hand combat. Lieutenant Richards drew his sword, trying to rescue Smitty. I tried to get to zee lieutenant, he ordered me to protect zee boy und ride back to Mar Musa to warn zee captain. He would hold them off for as long as he could to make sure Jäger and I could get away. I never saw a braver man. If it were not for Lieutenant

Richards, Jäger and I would be dead," he finishes, nodding to me to keep the lie.

"A great man, Lieutenant Richards," replies one of the officers. "You were lucky. If it was anyone else, you might have all perished."

"We could really use him now," Lieutenant York adds. "Tell me, Sergeant, who is this enemy?"

"Not sure. They looked like nomad raiders. A mercenary army of wogs serving zee Turks," Sergeant Sauer responds.

"Bold, very bold, to be attacking the King's Army," Lieutenant York muses.

"Wogs will die for a bit of gold. Wave some gold in a wog's face, and he will dance a jig which would make the Irish green with envy," says an officer who laughs alone.

It is a commonly held English belief that the Bedouin and Arabs, in general, are savages can be plied with gold to do anything; Lawrence offered gold to Prince Faisal[39] to secure the Bedouin allegiance to the King's Army. Hasan's father told me it was not gold that Prince Faisal and the Bedouin sought, however, but a nation free of the English, the French, and the Turks. The Bedouins want what we all want: independence. The gold is to buy weapons the English would not give them. The English have provided some guns, even a few Lewis guns, but artillery is something the English will not relinquish. It is well known that the Bedouins repeatedly ask for rolling artillery to fight against the Turks, but the English know that artillery is a crucial piece of kit—and one they would never wish to be pointed back at them if the Bedouins' allegiance turns. The Bedouins have secured some artillery, using gold the English gave them, and Prince Faisal also used the gold to buy the allegiance of some of the simpler Bedouin Tribes whose lust for gold blinds them.

The officers begin to disperse after finishing their breakfast.

"I have the watch. Glad to see you are better," says Ben. He gets up and is about to leave when he turns to Sergeant Sauer. "Thank you, Sergeant," he says.

* * *

When Sergeant Sauer and I are the only ones left at the table, he turns to me. "We must be careful, not to bring questions or suspicions. Honor Lieutenant Richards. He is English; I am not. Taking credit for something, which offers no benefit, does no one any good. It is better to play zee part they expect of you than to prove otherwise. Do you understand?"

I nod; I do understand what Sergeant Sauer is conveying. He wants us to not call attention to ourselves. We are at war with the Ottoman Empire; men are dying for what they believe in, and they need to trust their countrymen. Sergeant Sauer and I, on the other hand, are outsiders in this Great War. We are also facing another enemy—one that has not yet revealed itself—and it is best not to draw attention to that enemy until we know what we face and whom to trust.

"Now, *Herr* Jäger, let me show you zee art of zee blade." Sergeant Sauer pulls forth his knife, then spins and flips the knife in his palm, a skillful dance. "This vill be your most trusted ally. It vill not run out of bullets; it vill stop even zee largest man."

The blade is long, double-edged, the faded blue of hardened steel. The edge and tip are bright shiny silver, polished and sharp. The hilt looks like an antler. He notices my stare.

"Antler, from my last hunt … *Waldmannsart*,"[40] he says, looking at me.

I nod. Yes, my father taught me.

* * *

We head to the yard behind the large stone building now used as the main barracks. Sergeant Sauer finds a large piece of wood and begins to drag it. I can see his shoulder bothers him, so I help. We prop the wood against the stone wall and then the sergeant quickly turns and marches across the yard. I follow in anticipation.

"All knives have a weight und a balance. First, you must find zee center." Sergeant Sauer balances his knife on his finger. "Find zee balance." He flips the knife in the air and catches it in the same hand. Then, with the slightest movement and speed, the blade flies from his hand and sticks with a heavy thud into the wood, dead center. "*Herr* Jäger?"

He stares at me, and I understand I am to fetch the knife. I run and pull the knife from the wood. A couple of wiggles are required to break it free. I run back and hand him the blade, pommel first.

"Remember, always sharpen zee knife, especially after practice. Steel does not like zee bite of wood." I notice once again that the edge of the blade is shiny and sharp as a razor. "Find zee balance. Feel zee weight."

He hands me the knife, and I try to balance it like he did, but I drop the blade. "Sorry."

"Sorry is only for people who know better und have failed." He takes the knife from my hand and then places it in my hand correctly. "Hold zee blade like this. *Know* zee blade." He looks at me when he says this as if trying to will me this knowledge and then continues, "Once you know a blade, you should be able to throw a blade ... any blade."

Sergeant Sauer grabs the knife from my hand and shows me how to hold the blade for throwing. I watch it closely. The blade leaves his hand with speed, thudding heavily as it hits the target. Bull's-eye again. He nods. I know: Fetch the blade.

This time he hands me the knife, and I balance it. I hold it the way he shows me. I toss the blade ... and it smacks against the wood slab and falls to the ground.

"At least it hit zee target," the sergeant says. He laughs, the first time I have heard him laugh. He smiles and continues, "Practice. My shoulder bothers me. I go to zee doctor. *Herr* Jäger, do not leave until you can make zee knife stick, many times."

He starts to walk away. "How many times?" I ask.

He turns, looking puzzled.

"How many times in a row do I need to make sure it sticks in the wood?" I clarify.

He looks at me, then looks at the wood slab. He looks up toward the sun, then back at me. "Five times, then ten times, und then fifty times. You keep going until zee sun sets. When you cannot see zee wood, you do it some more. because you may not see zee wood, you know it is there und there vill be times when you need to hit zee target in zee dark." He turns and walks away.

Ridiculous, I think, but I spend the rest of the day throwing the knife and retrieving it.

As night falls, I calculate that I must have thrown the knife a thousand times. The motion begins to feel natural. My shoulder is sore, and my hand blisters, but I do not stop. Each time I throw the knife, I think about the night at the ruins of Shmemis: the bodies and blood. I do not want to succumb to death like Reynolds, Jones, Smitty, and Lieutenant Richards. I will not die at the hands of some cloaked enemy. I need to learn to defend myself. Sergeant Sauer is right—a day may come in which Spitz, my trusty Winchester, runs out of bullets, and then what?

18 Sergeant Sauer's Knife - F.M. Jäger (c. 1917)

CHAPTER 11

Captain Rat Face

It has been a couple of days since my knife practice, and I am feeling much better. Sergeant Sauer is also doing much better, although the cut was deep and he lost a lot of blood. The doctor has already stitched his wound closed a second time after Sauer tore the stitches. The doctor has ordered him to rest and let the wound heal, which only frustrates Sergeant Sauer. He is not a man who likes to rest. I visit him daily, and we take time in the yard, where I show him how my knife throwing has improved. He teaches me how to sharpen the knife to a razor's edge with a whetstone and leather strap.

"What's all the ruckus?" Ben inquires over breakfast.

"Townshend's boys—they've arrived!" explains Lieutenant York.

"Townshend's boys?" Ben asks.

"They are what's left of General Townshend's Sixth Poona Division, which never made it to Kut." Lieutenant York points to a rather short man with a sneering look about him. "That's the captain who was ordered to lead Lieutenant Richard's Section."

I can tell already that I do not like the captain. I was with a company of General Townshend's army when they retreated to Kut, and I wrote a story on the Siege of Kut. It was a bloody mess. I met General Townshend a couple of times, once during the siege.[41] He is an arrogant man, and his men had little faith in him. His surrender was a huge blow to the morale of the British Army. His men were force-marched across the desert and were beaten, shot, starved or died of thirst. It has been one of the greatest horror stories of the war. Rumors of General Townshend being an honored guest of the Ottoman Empire have made the whole affair worse, yet some still worship the general.

"Those Townshend boys are jack-arses of the King's Army. Send the lot of 'em home in a wood box, I say," an officer at the table huffs.

Twenty of the soldiers who have arrived are the remainder of General Townshend's division. The rest are what remains of Lieutenant Richard's Second Section. I can see they have experienced the full wrath of the Desert Sea, and of course, losing men in their skirmish with the Turks must have taken Fifth Company's morale to a new low.

Ben is eager to see a friend from Fifth Company and, hoping the friend had survived, rushes out to the courtyard. I follow.

Ben's friend, an enlisted boy from his hometown, has survived, and he shares the story of how the captain from General Townshend's division decided not to proceed across the desert, instead head north toward Damascus.

They ran into a Turkish division, sending Fifth Company's Second Section and the remainder of Townshend's men in full retreat. Fifth Company lost four men and had a dozen wounded. They regrouped at Salkhad and traveled through the Desert Sea to Mar Musa.

A large oaf of a sergeant from Townshend's division interrupts the boy's story. "What's ya snivilin' about? We got ya here."

"Not without losses!" Ben retorts.

"Stand to!" yells Lieutenant York. He walks up to the captain who led the remainder of Fifth Company's Second Section. "I'm sure you do not wish to keep the major waiting. Follow me."

The captain looks like a rat, with a permanent scowl on his face. He nods disrespectfully to Lieutenant York, and as he walks away, he turns and sneers at the men. "Behave yourselves; you're part of Townshend's Sixth Division, not a scallywag like this lot. Show them how a proper soldier behaves!"

* * *

A few minutes later, Lieutenant York locates me again in the officers' mess and orders me to report immediately to the commander's quarters.

"Sir," I say to announce my presence as I enter the room.

"A child?" screeches the crooked mouth of the captain of Townshend's Sixth Division. If ever a man alive looked to be the human offspring of a rodent, it must be Captain Rat Face.

"Mr. Jäger speaks fluent Arabic, as well as German, has traveled with the Bedouin, and has seen action. I think some respect is deserved," Major Bassett says firmly.

"Sure, sure." Captain Rat Face waves his hand dismissively toward the major. "So, tell me of this attack. You say dozens of them?"

"I'm sure Captain Wilson gave you a full report," I say.

"I read it and heard it again from Captain Wilson. Now I wish to hear it from you," he tells me. "I didn't ride across the desert to this hellhole for nothing, and I suspect this story of yours is just that … a *story* … after seeing Mr. Jäger is a mere child," he finishes, looking at the major and sneering as he says my name.

To end his insults, I interject as quickly as I can, "Our long-range patrol was attacked at night by twenty men. They killed both guards silently with knives, and Sergeant Sauer began to fire on the—"

"You mean our boche friend?" Rat Face asks sarcastically.

Disregarding him, I continue, "Sergeant Sauer began to fire, killing three instantly. He rushed to the aid of Lieutenant Richards, who fell in the battle, and he fought off two more as he rescued me."

"You mean he ran away from the battle with a child."

"Enough!" the major interrupts, having enough of Captain Rat Face's banter.

The captain raises his finger and points at Major Bassett. "Look here, Major; your reputation is none too good back at the front. Sure, you may have a friend or two in high places, but you command a bunch of misfits, shell-shocked good-for-nothings who ride *camels*! The only reason you were assigned this post was to save your family honor or name or some such nonsense, so you can go back to England and tell your lordly friends you were at the front and to show off some medals. I read the report and now see it is a child's story. And the only other survivor is a German soldier in the King's Army?"

The captain's rat eyes scan the room, and he shakes his little head in disgust. "No one wanted to come to this remote hellhole so far from the front, but you must still know someone, because I drew the short straw and was pulled from the front to figure out what all this fuss is over. I'm not part of the silly Camel Corps, but I agreed to lead your Fifth Company's Support Section north to this godforsaken place, and at the first sign of Turks, these camel boys of yours turned and ran. I have done my duty; I have delivered the rest of your Fifth Company camel boys!"

Captain Rate Face steps closer to the major, and Captain Wilson leans in as if to physically defend the major. Major Bassett stands stoically, raising his hand to calm Captain Wilson.

Rat Face's thin lips continue speaking in a hushed tone inches from the major. "You may be in command of these ruins you call a fort, but I command the men. I'll go look for your thieving nomads and hunt them down for you—if they existed at all. When I'm done, my men and I'll return to the front, where the real soldiers are winning this war!" He halts and then looks at Captain Wilson and me with disdain. Clapping his hands, he bellows, "Now, led me to this boche fellow. He's probably even more worthless than your lot, if the Imperial German Army doesn't want him."

"Captain Wilson, see to the watch and prepare for an assault," Major Bassett says. "I will take our friend here to see the sergeant."

Captain Wilson turns to leave, visibly upset by the confrontation, and the major, keeping his composure, tells Captain Rat Face, "Please, follow me."

As Captain Rat Face passes me, I inject, "Sergeant Sauer will confirm what I've said, these are dangerous—"

Before I can finish, Captain Rat Face pushes me against the wall. "Listen, snotty, you have not seen the real King's Army. The name Townshend is feared on the front, so keep your trap shut." His breath stinks, and spit hits my face as he speaks. He truly is a rat.

The major quietly shakes his head at me, to indicate that I am to leave it alone, and I follow Major Bassett and Captain Rat Face to the makeshift hospital to speak with Sergeant Sauer.

* * *

When we enter the hall, the major points to the door of Sergeant Sauer's room. Captain Rat Face pushes the major aside, opens the door to Sergeant Sauer's room forcefully, and freezes, staring at the scene in front of the window. The major and I step into the room behind him.

Sergeant Sauer's back is to us as he stares out the window into the courtyard, his massive frame blocking most of the window. A sunlight glow surrounds his upper torso, which is naked. Even though his chest is wrapped in a bandage, the sergeant's presence is still menacing. He is a giant, well over six feet. His massive shoulders flank his muscular back, which bears several deep scars of a brutal whipping from long ago. I count scars from at least four bullet holes in his back. It is an intimidating sight for anyone; the battle scars and physique tell a story no words can express.

Sergeant Sauer's voice is soft, his tone curt, as he says, "You must be zee captain of vat remains of Townshend's men vat did *not* fight at zee Siege of Kut!"

"Ahh, ahh, yeah. I came to get a ahh … ahh … first-hand account," squeaks Captain Rat Face.

Sergeant Sauer turns from the window and looks disapprovingly at Captain Rat Face. When he notices the major standing in the doorway, he snaps to attention, affording Major Bassett the respect he clearly is unwilling to bestow on Captain Rat Face.

"At ease, Sergeant," the major tells him.

"Sir, I trust all is well. I should be ready to report for duty today," Sergeant Sauer says, all but ignoring Captain Rat Face.

"Thank you, Sergeant Sauer. The captain would like to hear your report." Major Bassett nods toward Captain Rat Face. "Perhaps there is something you may wish to add?"

"Sir, I believe my report is complete, und I do not wish to speculate." Sergeant Sauer notices me and continues, "I believe zee person that can give you zee most accurate report, is *Herr* Jäger, his knowledge of zee region and his fluency in Arabic is excellent."

Captain Rat Face glares at me as he speaks to Sergeant Sauer. "We already have a report from the bo … ah … Mr. Jäger. I thought it would benefit from a detailed action report from a soldier."

"As I reported to Captain Wilson," Sergeant Sauer tells Captain Rat Face, "They are not Turks, not Ottomans, not Bedouins … und not *Germans*! They are well-trained Arab mercenaries willing to engage in hand-to-hand combat with soldiers."

"Sergeant Sauer, let me assure you Townshend's Sixth Division is the finest regiment in the King's Army serving in this theater of war."

Sergeant Sauer begins to smirk, enraging Captain Rat Face.

"And what do you find so amusing? You think the Imperial German Army is better?" Captain Rat Face snaps, his anger getting the better of him.

"I am sure General Townshend is relaxing in Istanbul, telling zee pasha of his great victories while his captured men enjoy their death march as they are whipped across zee desert!"

Captain Rat Face is red with anger. "General Townshend is the finest officer in His Majesty's Army and has fought with valor. It took twenty thousand Turks to take him. I dare say you should hold your tongue, as you have no idea to whom you are referring to—"

Major Bassett interrupts smoothly. "Captain, Sergeant Sauer served directly under General Townshend at the Siege of Kut. He's one of the few survivors who refused to surrender." It was rumored that when General Townshend gave the order to surrender, a handful of men

19 Sergeant Sauer - F.M. Jäger (c. 1917)

preferred to fight and die rather than surrender. Apparently, Sergeant Sauer was one of them.

An orderly from the command post enters Sergeant Sauer's room, saluting the major before handing the major a slip of paper. He salutes again, then exits.

We all look to the major as he reads the note aloud. "Townshend's Sixth Poona Division has been removed from the order of battle. Officers and men shall report immediately to their superior officers for reassignment. Full stop." The major looks at the arrogant Rat Face and repeats the order: "Captain, your division no longer exists. It says you should report to your immediate commanding officer for assignment."

Captain Rat Face turns red, then huffs loudly and bolts from the room.

* * *

" 'Whipped across the desert,' Sergeant?" Major Bassett asks, casting a disapproving look toward Sergeant Sauer.

"Zee truth is never too much, sir." Sergeant Sauer says respectfully.

"Yes, I've heard the stories too, and I know you had many friends die at Kut, as did I. He arrived too late with the remaining regiment of Townshend's Sixth Division to engage at Kut, lucky for him. Command warned me before he came. They needed to remove the captain from the front, as he is prone to not taking orders, typical of Townshend's subordinates. I needed to see for myself what kind of man he is. I do not believe he has ever fired a shot in battle, let alone led any men into battle. We got the men we need for the Fifth Company, but I need to figure out how best to manage this captain whose public worship of General Townshend will be his downfall and our greatest risk." The major's face grows thoughtful as he ponders how best to deal with this captain with a rat's face.

I am relieved to hear Major Bassett's words after Captain Rat Face disrespected him; I initially thought less of the major and his position, but he has proven me wrong. Apparently, the major knows precisely what he is doing as he schemes to utilize the remainder of General Townshend's men, perhaps adding them to Fifth Company.

"For now," Major Bassett tells us, "we let this captain play his game. If the men are prepared, I think we have a fighting chance. This captain underestimates everything, which is dangerous. Get better, Sergeant, and when you are ready, see Lieutenant York for assignment."

"Yes, sir!" Sergeant Sauer snaps to with a sharp salute.

Obviously, Sergeant Sauer has profound respect for the major, and that is good enough for me. Still, I need to know something.

"Major?" I ask.

The major turns to me with a raised eyebrow

"I must know ... You knew the Sixth Division was removed from the battle order before he arrived. You were just waiting ... right?"

Major Bassett winks and gives me a salute before exiting the room.

CHAPTER 12

Seekers of Death

There is a banging on my door. "Mr. Jäger, snap to! Commander's quarters on the double!" barks Lieutenant York.

"What's with Lieutenant Yoke at this bat's hour?" Ben whines from his bed, making fun of York's last name.

"Probably wants me to shine Captain Rat Face's boots!" I reply.

Ben pulls the covers over his head, wanting to catch a few more winks before his watch.

* * *

A short while later, Lieutenant York leads me to the command quarters and opens the door.

Major Bassett is there, along with Sergeant Sauer, Captain Wilson, and another officer I do not know. This other officer arrived with Captain Rat Face. The men are all concentrating on a map, discussing it in hushed voices.

As I enter, the major looks up. "Mr. Jäger, this is Lieutenant Robbins," he tells me, pointing to the officer I did not know.

Lieutenant Robbins looks up from the map and smiles. Sergeant Sauer gives me a nod as a signal.

All is good, I think. *Perhaps the major is to make his move now.*

"Our illustrious captain, who once led the remainder of Townshend's Sixth Poona Division, has informed me that he is planning two patrol sweeps, here and here," the major explains to me. "While it seems a decent plan, it is routine textbook and offers neither a counter nor retreat plan. He is giving our enemy an advantage by not considering them a threat. The patrols will be exposed and not able to cover their flank."

"Sergeant Sauer has mapped out the area. He's located outcroppings along the ridge to the east, here and here," Captain Wilson says, pointing to two marks on the map drawn in black wax.

"These positions offer cover fire and protection. From here, the patrol can retreat and resupply. Sergeant Sauer and Lieutenant York are going to supply and fortify these two locations tonight. It's a dangerous supply run but needs to be done before daybreak," continues the captain.

"I will be insisting our two patrols include Captain Wilson leading one of them," Major Bassett explains. "Sergeant Sauer and Lieutenant York will accompany them. Lieutenant Robbins will make sure to convince our visiting captain. The captain has no idea Lieutenant Robbins once served me—and well." The major rests a hand on Lieutenant Robbins's shoulder.

"Thank you, sir," Lieutenant Robbins says with a smile.

"As long as the patrols follow the sweeping maneuver, we will always be in short range of the two locations, and they can retreat if they must and also be well fortified with weapons and supplies." Captain Wilson sweeps his hand across the map near the two outcroppings.

I think it is a brilliant plan, but what am I supposed to do, and why is the plan being shared with me?

As if reading my mind, Major Bassett says, "Mr. Jäger, earlier this evening, we received a message from a passing Bedouin nomad. It's addressed to you. He said it is vital that you receive it as soon as possible. It's in Arabic. Please read it." He hands me the leather-wrapped scroll.

I look at Sergeant Sauer, and he nods. Does the nod mean I should share everything?

I open the leather bundle and unwrap the scroll to read. I read it quickly to myself while pretending to take time to decipher it.

Caecus,

My friend, British marched on Masyaf. Seekers search for Saladin's Hidayah. They believe the British have Saladin's Hidayah. Seekers will attack the British at Mar Musa. They will kill all the British. Seekers are willing to die. I and my brother are against my cousin; my cousin, and I are against the stranger.

Leave Now!

"Mr. Jäger?" The major's voice snaps me out of contemplation.

"Yes, sir, I'm sorry; some words are foreign to me."

"What does it bloody say?" Captain Wilson demands.

The major raises his hand to lower the tension, though I can tell he is concerned because we face an unknown enemy.

"It's a letter from a Bedouin I have traveled with. He heard I was attacked and is glad I'm safe. The letter says the enemy will attack the British at Mar Musa. He fears I'm not safe here. He tells me to leave for my safety."

"Is that all? What about the foreign part you don't understand?" asks Captain Wilson.

I do not want to share with him information about Saladin's Hidayah. I also did not recognize the name of the enemy. Reluctantly, I say, "I just have never heard this name before. I'm not exactly sure how to translate the name; I can only guess."

"What do you think it is?" inquires the major.

"I would translate it to Seekers of Life or Death."

"Sounds like a bloody wog cult," Lieutenant Robbins muses.

Major Bassett stares at me with a look of puzzlement as if he has heard this name before.

"It sounds familiar. I believe I heard it mentioned when I served on zee expedition before zee war," Sergeant Sauer replies, looking at me intensely.

I shared too much. It is undoubtedly a glare to stop talking at this point.

The major nods. "Yes, Sergeant, I have read the report on the expedition. The thought just crossed my mind, too, when Mr. Jäger mentioned it."

"Well, if they seek death, then we shall give it to them," Captain Wilson states. "Mr. Jäger, does it mention anything about their numbers, when they will attack, anything?"

"No, sir, only that they plan to attack the British at Mar Musa. There is no time or date, but it implies it would be soon."

"Do you think these Seeker folk are using Masyaf as a base of operations?" Captain Wilson asks.

Sergeant Sauer speaks up before I can reply. "I do not believe so, sir. They attacked us at Shmemis; it is at least one day from Masyaf. Zee attack on zee expedition vas further north. I believe zee Seekers tracked us from zee Roman Bath at Abu Rabah zee last two days of our patrol north." He points on the map to the base of the mountain where we had camped.

"Are you sure? That's two days' ride from Mar Musa. If they are there now, they could be upon us any day," Lieutenant York postulates.

Sergeant Sauer replies, "I did not observe them, I sense our patrol vas being tracked."

"Right. We will hold fast. The two patrols will sweep along the ridges near the supply dumps, and Lieutenant Robbins will secure Mar Musa." Major Bassett says, seemingly secure in the plan. "Mr. Jäger, do you have anything to add?" he asks.

"No, sir."

"Thank you. You're dismissed," he tells me with a nod and a smile. As I turn away, he returns his focus to the map; there is much to plan, and I am not to be engaged in the fight.

* * *

Before I reach the bottom of the stairs after leaving the command quarters, Sergeant Sauer catches up with me. Taking me by the arm, he pulls me into the shadows.

"Careful, *Herr* Jäger. Captain Wilson is a good man. He needs only to protect zee men. Zee Seekers are not after him; they seek zee dagger, Saladin's Hidayah, zee Secret."

"I know, but you heard, I didn't say anything. Who are these Seekers? Why didn't you tell me?"

"Now is not zee time, your friend instructed you to leave now and get away from here. Zee British Army has ventured into an ancient war. This is not part of their Great War."

"What war?"

"Your friend is right; this fort will fall, along with all zee British soldiers. You cannot let Saladin's Hidayah fall into their hands. It is not safe for you here."

"Then where?"

"Tomorrow, after zee patrol, I vill come back here and meet you at zee mess. Tomorrow evening we leave. Be ready at dusk; I vill have camels packed und vill lead them to zee other side of zee ravine. We vill take zee west ridge trail toward Al-Nabek. They vill not know we are gone until daybreak. This place vill fall, und best we are not here when it does."

Sergeant Sauer looks away, becoming distant as if remembering the past. "Zee translation is not 'Seekers of Life or Death.' It is 'Seekers of Life *from* Death.' " He leans closer and whispers, "They vill kill all, or be killed trying!"

He lets go of my arm and returns to the command post.

Knowing that I need to get ready, I head to the old building that serves as a bunkhouse. Ben is fast asleep. I grab my rucksack and Spitz. I do not feel safe; the moon is rising, meaning tomorrow will be upon us soon.

I decide I will sleep as I do in the open, where I feel safe. I walk down to where the camels rest. Tuff is there. She raises her head slightly, recognizing me. I glance at my watch, the glowing numbers painted on the dial indicating that it is after one o'clock in the morning. I hold the watch to my ear; still ticking. I wind the watch again, just to make sure.

I fall asleep to the tick-tick-tick of the watch clicking off the seconds until tomorrow.

CHAPTER 13

Rules of the Hunter

"Form up, form up! Stop ya skylarking … eyes front," Lieutenant York barks at the men who are mustering at daybreak. It has been my wakeup call since Mar Musa became my temporary home. I take comfort while observing from a distance, appreciating that I am not another regular in the King's Army.

Captain Rat Face marches out of the building he commandeered, flanked by his lackey, a good-for-nothing sergeant. The sergeant is a large oaf of a man, his muscle supporting the small bully who is Captain Rat Face. The flunky sergeant kicks one of the regulars as he passes, just to let him know who is in charge.

Captain Rat Face raises one hand in the air. "Pipe down and listen up. Some of you good-for-nothing men are going to learn some real soldiering. Captain Wilson and I are leading the patrols to sweep up these nomad thieves who have plagued you and killed your good Lieutenant Richards. Lieutenant Robbins made a wonderful suggestion to take a few of you with us to show you how proper patrollin' is done. Perhaps this time you won't all get yourselves killed. Lieutenant York, you will be under

Wilson's command. And my boche friend is with me—
yes, Sergeant Sour, zu are going to vride vith me." Captain
Rat Face said the last bit in a horrible German accent.

I hold my breath; no one calls him Sergeant Sour to
his face.

Sergeant Sauer steps forward, shoving Captain Rat
Face's lackey sergeant aside and towering over Rat Face.
There is a brief uncomfortable silence as the rest of us
wonder what he will do. Then Sergeant Sauer salutes and
barks, "Sir! I vill do my best to make sure you are safe
und avoid any situations in which you may consider sur-
rendering." It is a slight of epic proportions, as General
Townshend's surrender to the Turks is considered a stain
on the British Army. Several soldiers start chuckling.

Captain Rat Face ignores Sergeant Sauer, turning to
the men. "I'm going on this patrol to see what all this fuss
is about and to make sure you are no longer threatened
by these nomadic thieves with their little knives. We ride
out on the hour. The rest of you, Lieutenant Robbins will
show you how to prepare the fort for an attack—not that
we should expect anything after a couple of nomad thieves
are easily dispatched. We should be back before sunset,
and hopefully with some wog-head trophies to hang high!"

A couple of Townshend's boys cheer after the captain's
last words as if a wog's head is a grand trophy or a call to
battle.

I use the time before they leave to return Sergeant
Sauer's knife, which I have sharpened, and to have a private word with him.

"Thank you, *Herr* Jäger," Sergeant Sauer says as he
takes his knife from me. He slides it into the scabbard,

20 Captain Rat Face - F.M. Jäger (c. 1917)

which he has tied to his saddle for quick draw and use. Slapping the leather of the sheath, he tells me, "If you cannot get to it when you needed it, you might as vell not take it."

"Ahhhh, Sergeant Sour's houseboy delivering his supplies," rings Captain Rat Face's voice from behind me, and I turn to look at him. "Well, boy, if you have nothing left to do, I'm sure Lieutenant Robbins can assign you some duties, perhaps cleaning the latrine. Your sergeant will be back for dinner, and you can make his bed then. Now run along, snotty." He waves the back of his hand at me as if to shoo me away.

"Yes, sir, Captain Rat Face, sir! Anything you say, sir!" I snap back loudly, with an accompanying salute.

Everyone else in the courtyard begins to laugh. I guess I am not the only one who thinks the captain has a rat face. As I begin to turn and walk off, he tries to kick me in the ass but slips and falls on his own ass, which only causes further laughter in the courtyard.

"*Enough!* To your duties!" the major bellows from the top of the stairs. This is the first time I have heard his booming, commanding voice, which shakes every soldier to his core, even Townshend's boys.

I turn to see Sergeant Sauer offering his hand to help Captain Rat Face stand up, but the captain slaps the hand away. The captain stands up, humiliated, then dusts himself off and mounts his camel.

"Captain, Godspeed, and I trust you will prevail!" echoes the major's voice across the courtyard.

Captain Rat Face gives a half-assed salute, and the patrols leave down the path to the east.

Everyone can sense that the tables have finally turned; everyone, including Townshend's boys, know who is really in charge. After I humiliated Captain Rat Face in front of his own men, Major Bassett took the opportunity to rise above the pettiness and bring order. The mood at Mar Musa has changed, and for the positive—even hostilities between our men and Townshend's boys ease.

* * *

When you must wait, minutes feel like hours. I do not know how many times I glance at my watch or how many times I have wound it tight again. I am growing fidgety, and I have nothing to do as I wait for Sergeant Sauer and the patrols to return. I help clean up the mess hall, and then I visit Major Bassett.

"If you can't find something to do, I will find it for you!" the major snaps at me. Properly rebuked, I remind myself now is the time to wait and to trust in his men and his plan. He has far too much on his mind, and I am embarrassed at trying to seek surety—or is it comfort?

I walk the long hallway of the old stone building that acts as a barracks until I arrive at the yard where I practiced throwing Sergeant Sauer's trench knife. The wood slab leans against the wall, the center of the slab chewed up as if by a wild animal, the result of my target practice with the trench knife. My skills improved; I trace my finger over the marks in the slab. My thoughts turn to Sergeant Sawyer on patrol with Captain Rat Face.

I check Spitz for the third time or is it the fifth time. She is loaded; like she was the first time I check. I sling her over my shoulder and pat my pocket, a few extra bullets.

The church bell begins to ring. *The alarm!* Four slow clangs of the bell would signal wounded, whereas a non-stop rapid ringing means the men are to take battle stations. I hear the first ring and know the meaning before the next toll: wounded. My heart sinks. I stuff my rucksack, with Saladin's dagger, behind the wood slab and run to the gate.

One of the patrols is riding the trail slowly, looking battle-worn. Two dead men lay over the camels. No sign of Sergeant Sauer.

Captain Wilson dismounts and salutes Major Bassett.

"The captain's patrol fell under heavy attack. We rushed to their aid, and I ordered a retreat to the ridge we supplied, but the captain countered my order and told us to stand and fight. The enemy has rifles. Sergeant Sauer took command of their patrol after the captain fell. We retreated to the ridge and held them off. If we got there sooner, we may not have lost a man. Thankfully, sir, your plan of supplying the ridge with weapons was brilliant. I just wish we could have gotten there in time." Captain Wilson has a look of failure about him, his shoulders slumped.

"Not your fault, Captain, you did well. Where are Sergeant Sauer, our visiting captain, and the rest of the patrol?" The major's asks as his eyes scan the wounded.

Captain Wilson turns and nods toward the camels that have hauled the injured and dead. "Sergeant Sauer stayed behind with Lieutenant York to lay cover fire for us to escape with the wounded and dead, along with the captain. They were to follow but needed to make sure we were away safely."

Among the wounded is Captain Rat Face; he is unconscious, not dead. His oaf of a sergeant is among the dead. The major orders all the wounded to be taken to the hospital. "Lieutenant Robbins, sound the alarm. All able-bodied men to their stations. Prepare for an assault." Major Bassett heads to the command post, escorted by Captain Wilson.

The nonstop clanging of the bell is deafening and definitely alarming. It pauses only long enough for Lieutenant Robbins to yell, "To stations!" and then continues. Men scamper all over, half-dressed, grabbing guns and swords. It is an orderly panic.

Ben rushes out the door and calls to me. "This is it, Mare, a battle! We are going to see action!" He is eager and excited for this day he probably does not know he should never wish for.

I see him run off to the north wall, his station. I turn quickly; I need to grab my rucksack and, most importantly, Saladin's Hidayah. Sergeant Sauer is nowhere to be found, and if I must escape on my own, I need to make sure I have everything.

I run through the long hall of the barracks toward the yard where I hid my rucksack. A few stragglers are kitting up, grabbing weapons and rushing down the hallway. They completely ignore me, their adrenaline, like mine, pumping; the enemy can be upon us at any time.

I exit the barracks hall and scamper across the yard to the wooden slab. I pull it down, and the slab thuds as it hits the ground. My hand reaches into the rucksack and feels the wrapped bundle of Saladin's Hidayah.

Cracks of gunfire ring out, we are under attack. I sling the rucksack over my shoulder and rush across the yard into the hallway. I must cross the courtyard, to the back gate and find Tuff. If we can make it across the ravine to the west ridge trail, we can ride to Al-Nabek. Maybe Sergeant Sauer will meet us there. That was the plan.

I pause at the end of the hallway and scan the courtyard. The soldiers along the wall of the main gate are firing their rifles, the cracks of gunfire echo off the walls of the ravine. I can feel the panic and adrenaline of battle. I have been here before, as a reporter, it is a unique singular moment in a man's life. One's senses and focus are most acute, the mind wrestles with survival, fear, aggression, and panic. The exhilaration of battle is felt when the battle is won, now it is a pure survival instinct.

I am knocked to the floor by an echoing boom, my trance of the battle broken. I stand and look across the courtyard. The enemy has breached the front entrance, and one of the buildings has been blown apart by artillery. From the top of the stairs, the major is firing his gun into the enemy, who pour through the narrow entrance. I must get out of here. The cracks of gunfire ring in my ears as smoke fills the courtyard.

I dash across the courtyard to the back gate. Standing before me is the enemy, a Seeker dressed in a dusty dark robe, like the enemy we encountered at Shmemis. He is looking down at a fallen soldier but then turns and spots me. I drop my rucksack and raise Spitz into the familiar

21 Attack on Mar Musa 1917 - F.M. Jäger (c. 1917)

position my father taught me when we hunted for white-tailed deer.

My father's voice washes over me. *Waidmannsart, the rules of the hunter. Weak before strong, young before old. You are a part of the forest. Steady yourself. You are a tree, a rock. Your motion is fluid and quiet; it must be natural. The deer must see you as part of the forest. The eye on the target, the barrel aligns with the heart of the deer; the squeeze of the trigger is smooth and certain.*

As the barrel and my eye align on the target, I squeeze the trigger. Spitz erupts with an explosion of death. The enemy lifts off his feet and falls on his back as the .30-30 round hits him squarely in the chest. I slam the lever action, ejecting the hot shell and loading another.

The acrid stink of gunpowder fills my nose, and makes my eyes water. My lungs are raw! My ears ring, muting the cracks of gunfire and screams. I am unable to process what is happening; I have no muscle memory for battle.

I stand, frozen, staring at the man I have just shot. The blood is darker than I remember. Memories flood in, of a deer I killed: the deer's eyes, its gaze somehow forgiving, as life faded. The memory seems so far off, a lifetime ago. The man's eyes are the same … life begins to fade.

No, he is not a man, but a youth, not much older than myself. His hand grips an amulet around his neck. His lips quiver. A prayer?

"Mare!" a distance voice calls out.

I am Mare, I remember … or used to be, before I killed a man … a boy. What was his life like? His dreams? I bend down, unclench his fingers. The amulet hangs from a rawhide string. Without knowing why, I rip it free.

"*Mare!*" The voice is louder.

A hand grabs my shoulder. I wheel around, raising my rifle, ready to strike. I quickly lower my guard when I see it is my friend, my only friend in this hell on earth.

"We have to go. Now!" His voice is panic-stricken.

Still dazed, I nod. I look back at the boy I just killed, my first kill. Flies are buzzing in the blood. I slip the amulet into my pocket. The dark blood pools, ready to touch the tip of my boot. The thin line between life and death.

"Bloody hell," my friend says with alarm. "You've been shot!"

Only then do I become aware of the burning pain shooting up my arm. Blood trickles down. Red; I am still alive. My heart pounds so hard, my chest feels ready to burst. My ears stop ringing as time speeds up, and I hear screams, the firing of guns.

I turn and follow Ben into the fight. As I enter the courtyard, I realize I left my rucksack and the dagger. I turn and run back, past the body of the boy I just killed, grab my rucksack.

Everything goes dark.

The journey continues in
Destiny's War Part 2: Assassin Awakes

About the Author

Pyram King as a son of foreign exchange teachers, had become a world traveler by the age of 10. His travels took him into jungles and remote villages across South East Asia, on the Trans-Siberian Railway when China was ruled by Mao and the Soviet Union was a superpower, and sailed the Atlantic aboard the QEII. He experienced a coup and unrest in Central America, explored remote islands in the Pacific, climbed Kilimanjaro, and spent a volatile time in the Persian Gulf.

Traveling combined with his literary and adventurer inspirations; Burton, Lawrence, Hemingway, Hesse, became an essential defining part of his life, infusing a more profound interest in the history and culture of the places he visited.

Over the years he became an autodidact historian and economist, never satisfied with subjective answers and coincidences, he began his own research applying objective reasoning and logic. There were too many coincidences in history, too many stories thought to be nothing more than myths.

When others thought Homer's Iliad was nothing more than a myth, it was an amateur archeologist and businessman Schliemann who believe the text to be history, leading to the discovery of Troy. Despite Schliemann's criticized methods, the point was clear, there is far more to these ancient myths. One needs to dig, figuratively and sometimes literally.

Sometimes it takes an objective eye not molded by conventional wisdom to find the truth.

"Wisdom flows from the spring of experience and knowledge." ~ Sapiente

INDEX

To learn more, visit www.destinyswar.com

Characters (in alphabetical order)

Bassett, Major John (October 27, 1878 - 1958) Commander of the 2nd British Battalion. He is close friends with Captain Wilson and is well versed in ancient history.

ibn Faraj, Hasan Bedouin friend of Mare. A prince who has become a nomad fighter. Mare was adopted by Hasan's family before the war, and they became close friends before the war.

ibn Faraj, King Hasan's father and ruler of a Bedouin tribe that joins the Arab Revolt. Marion lives with their family before the war.

ibn Faraj, Roxana Hasan's sister and princess.

Jäger, Francis Marion, a.k.a. Mare, Caecus Narrator. Of Swiss German and American descent. His mother's great-uncle was Francis Marion (a.k.a., the Swamp Fox), who fought in the American Revolution. Father from Switzerland and was a hunter. Mother from a farming family. He ran away from home at fourteen years old after his mother died. He traveled to the Middle East, romantically fantasizing about the stories his mother told him about Sir Richard Francis Burton.

Jones "Dilberry" British soldier and a member of Lieutenant Richards's patrol to Masyaf; died at Shmemis.

Lawrence, T. E., a.k.a. Lawrence of Arabia (August 16, 1888 – May 19, 1935) British officer rumored to take Akaba with a group of Bedouin. Marion meets in the officer's mess.

Rat Face, Captain British captain of the remnants of General Townshend's Sixth Division. He leads Second Section of Captain Wilson's Fifth Company from Salkhad to Mar Musa. We do not learn his real name, Marion nicknames him Captain Rat Face.

Reynolds British soldier and a member of Lieutenant Richards's patrol to Masyaf; died at Shmemis

Richards, Lieutenant British officer, commands Second "Support" Section of Captain Wilson's 5th Company. Leads patrol to Masyaf; died at Shmemis

Robbins, Lieutenant British officer, arrived at Mur Musa under the command of Captain Rat Face, had previously served with Major Basset.

Sapiente the wise man and keeper of the scrolls; nick-named Muqla, or Muqla Daḵana by Marion. Had served King Faraj and was a teacher for Hasan, Roxana, and Marion.

Sauer, Sergeant a.k.a. Sergeant Sour, Ortis British Sergeant assigned to Lieutenant Richard's Second "Support" Section of Fifth Company. He is a member of Lieutenant Richards's patrol to Masyaf. A German soldier who fought in the Libyan War (1911–1912) and left for dead. Captured by the English, enlisted in British Army. His past is mysterious. He becomes friends with Marion.

Smith, Brigadier General Clement Leslie (January 17, 1878 – December 14, 1927) Commander of the Camel Corps. He is a friend of Ben Wright's father, who served with him before the Great War. Part of Ms. Bell's spy network. He assigns Marion his mission to Mar Musa.

Smitty British soldier and a member of Lieutenant Richards's patrol to Masyaf. Camp cook; died at Shmemis

Spitz nickname of Mare's Winchester 1894, a gift from his father; pronoun: *her*

Tuff Marion's camel acquired for the journey to Azraq.

Wilson, Captain Commander of the 5th British Company of the 2nd British Battalion. British officer serving directly under Major Bassett. He has an excellent rapport with his men and is a great field officer. Marion rode with him previously as a reporter in a previous battle.

Wright, Second Lieutenant Benjamin a.k.a. Ben British officer. He has just arrived in Egypt, assigned to command the Machine-gun Section of Captain Wilson's 5th Company of the Camel Corps. Marion meets him in the officer's mess in Kantara and joins him on his travels to Azraq to join Captain Wilson's 5th Company.

York, Lieutenant British Officer. Commands First Section of Capitan Wilson's Fifth Company. Leads a patrol that travels with Lieutenant Richard's patrol to Mar Musa. Marion becomes friends with Lieutenant York.

Locations (in alphabetical order)

Listed by their names and spellings from the early 19th century during World War I. Modern day location names are bracketed for reference. References in the Destiny's War Part 1: Saladin's Secret are *italicized*

A-Houl also known as the Terror, is a section of desert considered impassable, as no wells or other water is available for miles. *Rumors are that Lawrence crossed the A-Houl with Bedouins on his way to attack Akaba.*

Abu Rabah, Syria ruins consisting of Roman Baths.

Akaba, Jordan a city along the red sea. The site of the famous raid by T.E. Lawrence and the Arab Revolt.

Alawiyin Mountains are a mountain range in northwestern Syria, running north-south, parallel to the coastal plain.

Al-Nabek, Syria, a city on the banks of the Orontes River in west-central Syria, fifty miles north of Damascus.

Amman, Jordan the capital of Jordan.

Alamut Castle was a mountain fortress located in the Alamut region in the South Caspian province of Daylam. It was built by the Justanid ruler Wahsudan Marzuban around AD 865 after he witnessed a soaring eagle land on a high rock. Realizing the tactical advantage of this location, he chose the site for the construction of a fortress, which is called Alamut, "the Eagle's Nest." In AD 1090, Hassan-e Sabbāh, the leader of the Nizari Ismailis and the founder of the order known as Assassins, captured Alamut Castle. Alamut fell in 1256 to a Mongol invasion.

Azraq, Jordan a small town and ruins in central-eastern Jordan, 100 kilometers (62 miles) east of Amman. During the Arab Revolt in the early twentieth century, Qasr Azraq was an important headquarters for T. E. Lawrence. *Fifth Company, Second Battalion of the Imperial Camel Corps Brigade maintain a temporary base of operations. Mario and Ben travel from Rafah to Azraq, a five-day ride.*

Abbassia, Egypt used as a training camp for the Imperial Camel Corps during World War I. *Benjamin Wright is trained to ride a camel in Abbassia.*

Damascus, Syria the capital of Syria. A primary objective for the British forces during World War I. Initially controlled by the Ottoman Empire.

Dead Sea, Palestine [Israel] a salt lake bordered by Jordan to the east and Palestine to the west.

Deraa, Syria, a city in southwestern Syria, located about 13 kilometers (8.1 miles) north of the border with Jordan. Deraa means Fortress.

Druze, Syria also known as Jabal al-Druze, an elevated volcanic region in southern Syria.

El Qantara a.k.a. Kantara, Egypt (meaning "the bridge") a northeastern Egyptian city on both sides of the Suez Canal. A staging area for British and Allied forces during World War I. South of Port Said and north of Suez. *The newspaper office that Marion works for is in Kantara. He also visits the officer's mess.*

Euphrates is the longest, and one of the most historically important rivers of western Asia. Together with the Tigris, it is one of the two defining rivers of Mesopotamia ("land between the rivers").

Furqlus, Syria A village east of Homs. *Deserted after being raided by nomads. Turkish army controls the village, Marion and Sergeant Sauer stay a few hundred yards away on their retreat from Shmemis.*

Gaza, Palestine [Israel] a city along the Mediterranean Sea.

Hama, Syria a city on the banks of the Orontes River in west-central Syria.

Hejaz Railway was part of the Ottoman railway network. It was a narrow-gauge railway (1,050 millimeters, or 3 feet, 5 11/32 inches) that ran from Damascus to Medina, an important supply route for the Ottoman Empire during World War I. *Marion crosses the railway on his way to Azraq.*

Homs, Syria a city in western Syria.

Huwwarin, Syria A village north of Mar Musa, with old ruins outside of town, a day's ride from Mar Musa. *Marion and Sergeant Sauer stay in the ruins on their retreat to Mar Musa.*

Mar Musa, Syria, formally known as Deir Mar Musa al-Habashi ("the Monastery of Saint Moses the Abyssinian") is a monastic community of the Syriac Catholic Church located near the town of Nabk, approximately 80 kilometers (50 miles) north of Damascus. The main church of the monastic compound is home to precious frescoes dating to the eleventh and twelfth centuries. An ancient building, stone circles, lines, and tombs dating back 10,000 years were discovered in 2010 near the monastery. *Ruins are partially used by monks, Fifth Company uses the ruins as a secret base of operations.*

Masyaf Castle, Syria a castle in the town of Masyaf, Syria. Evidence suggests that the lower layers and foundations of the castle are of Byzantine origin or earlier. Later levels were added by the Nizari Ismailis, Mamluks, and Ottomans. The castle itself stands on a platform about 20 meters above the surrounding plain. The castle is captured by the Assassins in 1141 and is later refortified by Rashid al-Din Sinān. The citadel became famous as the stronghold from which Rashid ad-Din Sinān, known as the Old Man of the Mountains ruled. He is a leader of the Syrian wing of the Nizari Hashshashin sect, also known as the Assassins.

Mecca, Saudi Arabia the birthplace of Muhammad, and the site of Muhammad's first revelation of the Quran. *Marion mentions his pilgrimage to Mecca with Hasan.*

Medina, Saudi Arabia a city controlled by the Ottoman Empire and the last stop on the Hejaz Railway.

Mesopotamia a historical region of western Asia situated within the Tigris–Euphrates river system, in the northern part of the Fertile Crescent, in modern days roughly corresponding to most of Iraq, Kuwait, the eastern parts of Syria, southeastern Turkey, and regions along the Turkish–Syrian and Iran–Iraq borders.

Rafah, Palestine [Egypt] A city on the border between Egypt and Palestine. Sinai Military Railway stopped here, and the city was used during part of World War I as a forward supply and staging area. Marion and Ben take the train from Kantara to Rafah. *Marion arrives in Rafah with Ben on the train. Marion acquires Tuff from a Bedouin merchant.*

Rhube Oasis, Syria An oasis northeast to Salkhad on the edge of the Syrian Desert. *Marion and the patrols stop to fill up water and rest before the desert crossing. Two days ride from Salkhad.*

Salkhad, Syria a city consisting of the Salkhad Fortress built by the Ayyubid dynasty between 1214 and 1247 to defend against Crusaders. *Marion and 5th Company* *travel north from Azraq to Salkhad as a temporary base of operations.*

Sea of Galilee, Palestine [Israel] is a freshwater lake.

Shmemis, Syria a castle located thirty kilometers southeast from Hama. Built on top of an extinct volcano in the first century BCE. *Lieutenant Richards's long-range patrol stays the night before advancing to Masyaf. They are attacked, Marion and Sergeant Sauer retreat to Mar Musa. It is a three to four-day journey from Mar Musa to Shmemis.*

Sinai, Egypt a peninsula in Egypt, the only part of the country located in Asia. It is situated between the Mediterranean Sea to the north and the Red Sea to the south and is a land bridge between Asia and Africa. *Marion crosses the Sinai by train from Kantara to Rafah.*

Sinai Military Railway a railway built by the British forces from Kantara to Rafah during World War I. *Marion travels with Ben to Rafah aboard the train.*

Syrian Desert, Syria a.k.a. Desert Sea. The Syrian Desert, also known as the Syrian steppe, the Jordanian steppe, or the Badia, is a region of desert, semi-desert, and steppe covering 500,000 square kilometers (200,000 square miles) of the Middle East. *Marion and the patrol cross the desert and circle around Damascus to Mar Musa.*

Zir'in, Palestine [Israel] is a village identified as the ancient town of Yizre'el (Jezreel) mentioned by Joshua in the Bible. Yizre'el translates in Hebrew as "God give seed," from a common Canaanite root meaning to sow. Its Arabic name, Zir'in, has a similar connotation. *Saladin hides the dagger in the abandon crusader castle in Zir'in.*

Imperial Camel Corps Brigade (ICCB)

1916–1919
Commander: Brigadier General Leslie Clement Smith
The strength of the brigade/corps in the field approximately 4150 men and 4,800 camels (late 1917)

Organization

Battalion (770 men) (4 companies)
- **Company** (184 men) (6 sections)
- **Command Section** (40 men)
- 4x **Rifle Section** (32 men) (8 Groups)
- 1x **Machine-gun Section** (15 men) (3 Lewis guns)

Four-man group was the smallest level of organization unit in the camel companies.

Order of Battle 1917

- ✧ Brigade Headquarters (40 men)—**Brigadier General Smith**
- ✧ First Battalion (770 men)
- ✧ **Second (British) Camel Battalion—Major Basset (770 men)**
  - o **Fifth Company—Captain Wilson (185 men)**
    - *First Section—Lieutenant York (32 men)*
    - *Second "Support" Section—Lieutenant Richards (32 men)*
    - *Machine-gun Section—Second Lieutenant Wright (15 men)*

- Third Camel Battalion (770 men)
- Fourth Camel Battalion (770 men)
- Hong Kong and Singapore (Mountain) Battery (255 men)
- 265th (Camel) Machine Gun Squadron (115 men)
- Tenth (Camel) Field Troop, Royal Engineers (71 men)
- Signal Section, ICC Brigade (30 men)
- Australian (Camel) Field Ambulance (185 men)
- Ninety-seventh Australian Dental Unit (4 men)
- ICC Mobile Veterinary Section (42 men)
- ICC Brigade Ammunition Column (75 men)
- ICC Brigade Train (245 men)

Camel

In the desert a camel can routinely go up to five days without water.

The walking pace of the camels used by the Imperial Camel Corps was on average calculated to be 4.8 km (3 miles) an hour. At a trot they could make 9.5 km (6 miles) an hour. Daily operational range of a company was between 20 to 50 miles.

Each camel was expected to carry a load of at least 145 kg (the average weight of a cameleer, his equipment and supplies—which included 300 rounds of .303 ammunition for his rifle).

World War I Campaigns and Battles

Referenced in Destiny's War Part 1: Saladin's Secret

Date Ordered

The Gallipoli Campaign (February 17, 1915 – January 9, 1916) took place on the Gallipoli peninsula. Allied forces launched a naval attack followed by an amphibious landing at Gallipoli, with the aim of capturing Constantinople (modern Istanbul), the Ottoman Empire's capital. The Allied naval attack was repelled, and the Allied forces at Gallipoli took heavy casualties. The Allies retreated, withdrawing to Egypt. The campaign was a major victory for the Ottoman Empire. In Turkey, the battle is regarded as a defining moment in the nation's history, a final surge in defense of the motherland as the Ottoman Empire crumbled. Even though the Allies retreated, the Australian and New Zealand forces fought with such bravery and courage, they became highly respected among the Allied forces, as well as feared by the Ottomans. The campaign is often considered to be the beginning of Australian and New Zealand national consciousness; 25 April, the anniversary of the landings, is known as ANZAC Day, the most significant commemoration of military casualties and veterans in the two countries, surpassing Remembrance Day (Armistice Day).

The Siege of Kut (December 7, 1915 – April 29, 1916), also known as the First Battle of Kut, was the siege of a British-Indian garrison in the town of Kut, 160 kilometers (100 miles) south of Baghdad, by the Ottoman army. Suffering staggering losses, over 30,000 dead or wounded, General Townshend arranged a ceasefire on 26 April and, after failed negotiations, simply surrendered on 29 April 1916 after a siege of 147 days. Over 13,000 Allied soldiers survived to be made prisoners. The prisoners were sent on a death march, in which 65–70 percent of the British troops and 15–30 percent of the Indian troops died of disease or at the hands of their Ottoman guards. Townshend himself was taken to the island of Heybeliada, on the Sea of Marmara, to sit out the war in relative luxury. The Siege of Kut is considered the worst defeat of the Allies in World War I.

The Battle of the Somme (July 1 – November 18, 1916) was fought by the armies of the British Empire and France against the German Empire. It took place on both sides of the upper reaches of the River Somme in France. The battle was intended to hasten a victory for the Allies and was the largest battle of World War I on the Western Front. More than three million men fought in the battle, and one million men were wounded or killed, making it one of the bloodiest battles in human history.

Battle of Rafah (January 9, 1917) Third battle to complete the recapture of the Sinai Peninsula by British forces during the Sinai and Palestine Campaign of World War I.

The Raid on Nekhl (February 1917) was the second of three battles in which British forces tried to recapture the Sinai Peninsula during the Sinai and Palestine Campaign of World War I. Egyptian Expeditionary Force (EEF) mounted forces traveled into the center of the Sinai Peninsula to attack and push the last Ottoman army garrisons back into Palestine.

The Battle of Akaba (July 6, 1917) was fought for the Red Sea port of Akaba (now in Jordan). The attacking forces of the Arab Revolt, led by Auda ibu Tayi and advised by T. E. Lawrence (also known as Lawrence of Arabia), were victorious over the Ottoman defenders. The Arab Revolt expedition started moving toward Akaba in May 1917, crossing the al-Houl, considered an unpassable part of the desert. Auda ibu Tayi and his men reached the Wadi Sirhan region. At one point in this expedition, he went on a solitary reconnaissance mission, destroying a railroad bridge. Lawrence did this largely to convince the Turks that the Arab force was moving toward Damascus or Aleppo rather than toward Akaba. The battle for Akaba began at Abu al Lasan, about halfway between Akaba and the town of Ma'an. A group of Arab rebels, acting in conjunction with Lawrence's Arab Revolt expedition, had seized the fortification a few days before, but a Turkish infantry battalion arrived on the scene and recaptured it. The Turks then attacked a nearby encampment of Arabs and killed them. Auda ibu Tayi personally led the successful counterattack on the Turkish troops on 2 July 1917. In all, 300 Turks were killed and another 300 taken prisoner, compared to two Arabs killed and a handful wounded. Lawrence was nearly killed in the action; Auda ibu Tayi was grazed numerous times. Lawrence, ibu Tayi, and Nasir had rallied their troops; their total force had risen to 5,000 men thanks to local Bedouin who, after the defeat of the Turks at Abu al Lasan, openly joined ibu Tayi's force. This force maneuvered past the outer works of Akaba's defensive lines and approached the gates of Akaba, where the city's garrison surrendered without further struggle.

Ancient Battles

Referenced in Destiny's War Part 1: Saladin's Secret

Date Ordered

Siege of Masyaf (1176) Saladin faced a threat from the Ismaili sect known as the Assassins, led by Rashid ad-Din Sinān. Based in the an-Nusayriyah Mountains, the Assassins commanded nine fortresses, all built on high elevations. Saladin led his army into the an-Nusayriyah range in August 1176 and besieged Sinān's castle at Masyaf. Saladin retreated the same month, after laying waste to the countryside but failing to conquer any of Sinān's forts. Viewing the expulsion of the Crusaders as a mutual benefit and priority, Saladin and Sinān maintained cooperative relations afterward, with Sinān dispatching contingents of his forces to bolster Saladin's army in a number of decisive subsequent battles.

Battle of Al-Fule (1183) (La Fève to the Crusaders; *Castrum Fabe* in Latin), a Crusader force led by Guy of Lusignan skirmished with Saladin's army for more than a week in September and October 1183. The fighting ended on 6 October with Saladin choosing to withdraw.

Ain Jalut (1260) also known as "Spring of Goliath" or "Harod Spring." The Battle of Ain Jalut (AD 1260) was a battle between Muslim Mamluks and the Mongols in southeastern Galilee, in the Jezreel Valley, not far from the site of Zir'in. Sultan Qutuz was allied with Baibars in the face of a greater enemy after the Mongols captured Damascus.

Glossary

Allied forces the term commonly used for the Allies of World War I or the Entente Powers—the coalition that opposed the Central Powers of Germany, Austria-Hungary, the Ottoman Empire, and Bulgaria during World War I (1914 – 1918). The Entente Powers, also known as the Triple Entente, was made up of France, the United Kingdom, and Russia, the major European powers. The United States joined as an "associated power" rather than an official ally. Other "associated powers" included Serbia, Belgium, Greece, Montenegro, and Romania.

ANZAC (The Australian New Zealand Army Corps) was a World War I army corps of the Mediterranean Expeditionary Force.

Bedouin are tribes of nomadic Arab people who have historically inhabited the desert regions in North Africa and the Middle East.

Camel Corps formally known as the **Imperial Camel Corps Brigade (ICCB)** is a camel-mounted infantry brigade that the British Empire raised in December 1916 during World War I for service in the Middle East. The ICC became part of the Egyptian Expeditionary Force (EEF) and fought in several battles and engagements, in the Senussi Campaign, the Sinai and Palestine Campaign, and in the Arab Revolt. The brigade suffered 246 men killed. The ICC is disbanded in May 1919 after the end of the war.

Crusaders were warriors who fought for the Church during the Crusades, a series of religious wars sanctioned by the Latin Church in the medieval period.

Enfield, a.k.a. **Lee–Enfield**, was a bolt-action magazine-fed repeating rifle that served as the main firearm used by the military forces of the British Empire and Commonwealth during the first half of the twentieth century. It was the British Army's standard rifle from its official adoption in 1895 until 1957. The Lee–Enfield was adapted to fire the .303 British service cartridge, a rimmed, high-powered round. World War I versions of the Enfield are often referred to as the SMLE, short for "Short Magazine Lee-Enfield." The bolt-action and ten-round magazine capacity enabled a well-trained rifleman to perform the "mad minute," firing twenty to thirty aimed rounds in sixty seconds, making the Lee–Enfield the fastest military bolt-action rifle of the day. The current world record for aimed bolt-action fire was set in 1914 by a musketry instructor in the British Army—Sergeant Instructor Snoxall—who placed thirty-eight rounds into a twelve-inch-wide (300 millimeter) target at 300 yards (270 meters) in one minute. World War I accounts tell of British troops repelling German attackers, who subsequently reported that they had encountered machine guns, when in fact it was simply a group of well-trained riflemen armed with SMLE rifles.

"Golden Age of Cricket" a nostalgic term that has often been applied in cricket literature to the period in English cricket from 1890, the opening season of the official County Championship, to the outbreak of World War I, which occurred just before the scheduled end of the 1914 season.

Knights Templar, or simply the Templars, were a Catholic military order founded in 1119 and active until 1312.

Lord's Cricket Ground, commonly known simply as Lord's, is a cricket venue in St John's Wood, London.

Mess or officers' mess is an area where military officers socialize and eat.

Oasis the combination of a human settlement and a cultivated area (often a date palm grove) in a desert or semidesert environment. Oases also provide habitat for animals and other plants.

Omega a watch manufacturer. The early "trench watch" was a pocket watch modified to be worn on the wrist.

Ottoman Empire, a state that controlled much of Southeast Europe, Western Asia, and North Africa between the fourteenth and early twentieth centuries.

Pincer movement a military maneuver in which forces simultaneously attack both flanks (sides) of an enemy formation.

Sixth (Poona) Division was a division of the British Indian Army that, served in the Mesopotamian campaign, led by Major General Townshend.

Springerle a type of German cookie with an embossed design made by pressing a mold onto rolled dough and allowing the impression to dry before baking. This preserves the detail of the surface pattern. Historical molds show that springerles were baked for seasonal celebrations, perhaps pagan. Molds typically were of natural elements: flowers, trees, horses, and birds. They are now most commonly associated with the Christmas season. The word springerle translates literally as "little jumper" or "little knight," but its exact origin is unknown. It has been suggested that the name refers to "rising" in the context of celebrating the spring equinox.

Stone an English measurement commonly used to measure body weight, one stone = fourteen pounds.

Tamarind a tree that produces pod-like fruit that contains an edible pulp used in cuisines around the world.

Vickers a heavy belt-feed machine-gun

Waldmannsart a collection of centuries-old traditions and rules that a German hunter needs to follow. Literal translation "forest man's kind"

Winchester Model 1894 rifle (also known as the Winchester 94 or Model 94) a lever-action repeating rifle, one of the most famous and popular hunting rifles of all time. Designed by John Browning in 1894, it was the first rifle to chamber the smokeless powder round, the .30 WCF (Winchester Center Fire, in time, becoming known as the .30-30) in 1895. The rifle was produced from 1894 to 2006. One Model 1894 is on display at the Metropolitan Museum of Art in the Arms & Armour department.

Bedouin and Arabic References

Al-Ḥashāshīn also known as **Assassins**, is the name given to the Nizari Ismailis in the mountains of Syria between about 1090 to 1275. Nizarism formed in the late 11th century after a split within Ismailism, a branch of Shia Islam. The disciples were called Asāsiyyūn meaning "people who are faithful to the foundation. Marco Polo misunderstood the name as deriving from the term hashish, which began the myth the name Assassin derived from hash smokers. The Assassins posed a strategic threat to Sunni authority by capturing and inhabiting several mountain fortresses, including Masyaf. Asymmetric warfare, psychological warfare, and surgical strikes were often a tactic of the assassins, drawing their opponents into submission rather than risk killing them. While "Assassins" typically refers to the entire sect, only a group of acolytes known as the Fedayeen engaged in assassinations.

Alamut means "eagle's nest."

Asil from the concept of *Asalah*, meaning pure and authentic. Asil is a commonly referred-to breed of Arabian Horse.

Hamasa (courage/bravery) also closely linked to *sharaf*. Bravery indicates the willingness to defend one's tribe for the purpose of aṣabīya (tribal solidarity and balance) and is closely related to muruwa (manliness). It usually entails the ability to withstand pain.

Hidayah literal translation "guidance."

"I am against my brother; my brother and I are against my cousin; my cousin and I are against the stranger," sometimes quoted as "I and my brother are against my cousin; I and my cousin are against the stranger," is a Bedouin apothegm signifying a hierarchy of loyalties based on the proximity of male kinship. Disputes are settled, interests are pursued, and justice and order are dispensed and maintained by means of this framework, organized according to an ethic of self-help and collective responsibility.

Ma'a salama good-bye, literal translation "with safety".

Qiyamah literal translation "resurrection", is the belief in the resurrection of the people, whether Muslim or not, on the Day of Judgment.

Sāḥib a word of Arabic origin meaning "companion." In English, it is especially associated with British rule in India. It can be used as a term of address, either as an official title or an honorific.

Sharaf the general Bedouin honor code for men. Honor can be acquired, augmented, lost, and regained. *Sharaf* involves protection of the *ird* (honor code for women) of the family, protection of property, and maintenance of the honor of the tribe and protection of the village.

Wadi the Arabic term referring to a dry riverbed that contains water only when heavy rain occurs.

Slang and Idioms

Argy-bargy an argument or fight

Bit of stick to fight, giving a hard time, roughing up

Bloody an intensifier to show anger

Boche a disparaging British epithet for Germans

Clinker a jail

Cock robin a soft or weak man

Dilberry small pieces of excrement adhering to the hairs near the fundament

Dough-boy American soldiers in World War I

Paddy silly

Poof a derogatory word for homosexual

Poppycock senseless talk; nonsense

Ramshackle broken-down, rickety

Stiff an alcoholic drink

Scrumpy a drink

Tin a plate, usually metal used in the military

Wog usually employed as an ethnic or racial slur

Table of Figures

Endnotes

1. **The assassination of Archduke Ferdinand** in Sarajevo precipitated Austria-Hungary's declaration of war against Serbia, which in turn triggered a series of events that resulted in Austria-Hungary's and Serbia's allies declaring war on each other, starting World War I.

2. **The Gallipoli Campaign** (February 17, 1915 - 9 January 9, 1916) took place on the Gallipoli peninsula. Allied forces launched a naval attack followed by an amphibious landing at Gallipoli, with the aim of capturing Constantinople (modern Istanbul), the Ottoman Empire's capital. The Allied naval attack was repelled, and the Allied forces at Gallipoli took heavy casualties. The Allies retreated, withdrawing to Egypt. The campaign was a major victory for the Ottoman Empire. In Turkey, the battle is regarded as a defining moment in the nation's history, a final surge in defense of the motherland as the Ottoman Empire crumbled. Even though the Allies retreated, the Australian and New Zealand forces fought with such bravery and courage, they became highly respected among the Allied forces, as well as feared by the Ottomans. The campaign is often considered to be the beginning of Australian and New Zealand national consciousness; April 25th, the anniversary of the landings, is known as ANZAC Day, the most significant commemoration of military casualties and veterans in the two countries, surpassing Remembrance Day (Armistice Day).

3. **The Siege of Kut** (December 7, 1915 – April 29, 1916), also known as the First Battle of Kut, was the siege of a British-Indian garrison in the town of Kut, 160 kilometers (100 miles) south of Baghdad, by the Ottoman army. Suffering staggering losses, over 30,000 dead or wounded, General Townshend arranged a ceasefire on 26 April and, after failed negotiations, simply surrendered on April 29 1916 after a siege of 147 days. Over 13,000 Allied soldiers survived to be made prisoners. The prisoners were sent on a death march, in which 65–70 percent of the British troops and 15–30 percent of the Indian troops died of disease or at the hands of their Ottoman guards. Townshend himself was taken to the island of Heybeliada, on the Sea of Marmara, to sit out the war in relative luxury. The Siege of Kut is considered the worst defeat of the Allies in World War I.

4. **Thomas Edward Lawrence, CB, DSO** (August 16, 1888 – May 19, 1935), also known as T. E. Lawrence, was a British archaeologist, army officer, diplomat, and writer renowned for his liaison role during the Sinai and Palestine Campaign and the Arab Revolt against the Ottoman Empire during World War I. The breadth and variety of his activities and associations, and his ability to describe them vividly in writing, earned him international fame as Lawrence of Arabia, a title used for the 1962 film based on his wartime activities. In the summer of 1909, he set out alone on a three-month walking tour of crusader castles in Ottoman Syria, during which he traveled 1,000 miles (1,600 kilometers) on foot. In December 1910, he sailed for Beirut and on his arrival went to Jbail (Byblos), where he studied Arabic. He then went to work on the excavations at Carchemish, near Jerablus in northern Syria, where he worked under Hogarth, R. Campbell Thompson of the British Museum, and Leonard Woolley until 1914. While excavating at Carchemish, Lawrence met Gertrude Bell.

5. **Francis Marion** (c. 1732 – February 27, 1795) was a military officer in the American Revolutionary War (1775–1783). He used irregular methods of warfare and thus is considered one of the fathers of modern guerrilla warfare and maneuver warfare. He is also credited in the lineage of the US Army Rangers.

6. **The Imperial Camel Corps Brigade (ICCB)** is a camel-mounted infantry brigade that the British Empire raised in December 1916 during World War I for service in the Middle East. The ICC became part of the Egyptian Expeditionary Force (EEF) and fought in several battles and engagements, in the Senussi Campaign, the Sinai and Palestine Campaign, and in the Arab Revolt. The brigade suffered 246 men killed. The ICC is disbanded in May 1919 after the end of the war.

7. **Major John Retallack Bassett** (October 27, 1878 – 1958) served as Acting Chief Staff Officer with the Royal Berkshire Regiment during the Boer War and was appointed Governor of the Province of Sudan on 25 October 1916, where he became a trusted member of General Reginald Wingate's inner circle. Following this, he took up an important role as an intelligence liaison officer with the French in the eastern Mediterranean, working closely with the British Eastern Mediterranean Special Intelligence Bureau and then placed in command of the Second Battalion, Imperial Camel Corps in Sinai on 23 January 1917. Bassett was a close confidant of TE Lawrence and was mentioned in Seven Pillars of Wisdom as a key player in helping Lawrence and the Arab Revolt.

8. **The Raid on Nekhl** (February 1917) was the second of three battles in which British forces tried to recapture the Sinai Peninsula during the Sinai and Palestine Campaign of World War I. Egyptian Expeditionary Force (EEF) mounted forces traveled into the center of the Sinai Peninsula to attack and push the last Ottoman army garrisons back into Palestine.

9. **Abbassia** city in Egypt used as a training camp in World War I.

10. **The Ottoman Empire**, a state that controlled much of Southeast Europe, Western Asia, and North Africa between the fourteenth and early twentieth centuries.

11. **Stone** is an English measurement commonly used to measure body weight, one stone = fourteen pounds.

12. **The Hejaz railway** was part of the Ottoman railway network. It was a narrow-gauge railway (1,050 millimeters, or 3 feet, 5 11/32 inches) that ran from Damascus to Medina, an important supply route for the Ottoman Empire during World War I.

13. **Sir Richard Francis Burton** (March 19, 1821 – October 20, 1890) was a British explorer, geographer, translator, writer, soldier, cartographer, ethnologist, spy, linguist, poet, fencer, and diplomat. He was also a fellow of the Royal Geographical Society. Burton is famed for his travels and explorations in Asia, Africa, and the Americas, as well as for his extraordinary knowledge of languages and cultures. He spoke twenty-nine languages. The first known westerner to make the hajj to Mecca (in disguise), he documented his journey. He translated and published *One Thousand and One Nights* and the Kama Sutra. Along with John Hanning Speke, he was the first European to visit the Great Lakes of Africa in search of the source of the Nile.

14. **Brigadier General Clement Leslie Smith,** VC, MC (January 17, 1878 - December 14, 1927) was a British Army officer and a recipient of the Victoria Cross, the highest award for gallantry in the face of the enemy that can be awarded to British and Commonwealth forces. He commanded the Camel Corps during World War I.

15. **The German Intelligence Bureau for the East** (*Nachrichtenstelle für den Orient*) was a German intelligence organization established on the eve of World War I, dedicated to

promoting and sustaining subversive and nationalist agitations in the British Indian Empire and the Persian and Egyptian satellite states. Attached to the German Foreign Office, it was headed by archaeologist Baron Max von Oppenheim. Oppenheim was replaced in 1915 by Schabinger von Schowingen, who was replaced in 1916 by Eugen Mittwoch. In its initial period, the bureau was intricately involved in almost all the events that ultimately came to be called the Hindu–German Conspiracy, including the Annie Larsen plot, Ghadar conspiracy, Siam–Burma plan, attempts in Bengal, and other lesser-known plots in the Near East, including in Afghanistan and of the western borders of British India. In addition to its subversive campaigns against British possessions in India, the bureau also attempted to instigate instability in British possessions in the Muslims in India as well as around the world, in the Middle East, and in Egypt. It was involved in early Turkish plans for war and in the caliph's decision to declare jihad. The bureau was involved in intelligence and subversive missions to Persia and Afghanistan, and it also attempted, along with the Berlin Committee, to recruit Indian soldiers in Mesopotamia.

16. **Max von Oppenheim** (July 15, 1860 – November 17, 1946) was a German ancient historian, and archaeologist, as well as the head of the German Intelligence Bureau of the East from the start of the war until 1915. He was also a member of the Oppenheim banking dynasty. He discovered the historical ruins of Tell Halaf in 1899 and excavated them in 1911–1913 and again in 1929. After serving as the head of German intelligence in 1915, Oppenheim's whereabouts were unknown. Reports from British intelligence stated he had been traveling with Arabs, encouraging uprising against the British and French. Oppenheim's official account begins again in 1922 after the war, when he became a private scholar and founded the *Orient-Forschungsinstitut,* an institute for advanced study in Middle Eastern culture and history.

17. **Gertrude Margaret Lowthian Bell, CBE** (July 14, 1868 – July 12, 1926) is an English writer, traveller, political officer, administrator, and archaeologist who explored, mapped, and became highly influential to British imperial policy-making due to her knowledge and contacts, built up through extensive travels in Greater Syria, Mesopotamia, Asia Minor, and Arabia. Along with T. E. Lawrence, Bell helped support the Hashemite dynasties in what is today Jordan as well as in Iraq. She played a major role in establishing and helping administer the modern state of Iraq, utilizing her unique perspective from her travels and relations with tribal leaders throughout the Middle East. During her lifetime, she is highly esteemed and trusted by British officials and exerted an immense amount of power. She has been described as "one of the few representatives of His Majesty's Government remembered by the Arabs with anything resembling affection." At the outbreak of World War I, Bell's request for a Middle East posting is initially denied. She instead volunteered with the Red Cross in France. Later, she is asked by British Intelligence to get soldiers through the deserts, and from World War I period until her death she is the only woman holding political power and influence in shaping British imperial policy in the Middle East. She often acquired a team of locals, which she directed and led on her expeditions. Throughout her travels, Bell established close relations with tribe members across the Middle East. Additionally, being a woman gave her exclusive access to the chambers of wives of tribe leaders, giving her access to other perspectives and functions.

18. **Kim (Kimball O'Hara},** an orphan boy and spy, is the main character in the novel *Kim* by English journalist, short-story writer, poet, and novelist **Rudyard Kipling** (30 December 1865–18 January 1936).

19. **Lord's Cricket Ground**, commonly known simply as Lord's, is a cricket venue in St John's Wood, London.

20. **Vickers** is a heavy belt-feed machine-gun

21. **Colin Blythe** (May 30, 1879 – November 8, 1917), also known as Charlie Blythe, was an English first-class cricketer active from 1899 to 1914. He played in nineteen Test matches for England from 1901 to 1910. He is one of the five Cricketers of the Year named in the 1904 edition of *Wisden Cricketers' Almanack* and is generally regarded as one of the greatest bowlers in cricket history. Blythe is one of only thirty-three players who has taken 2,000 wickets in a first-class career. In 1917, because of heavy losses in the Battle of the Somme, British authorities encouraged charity cricket matches to boost morale. On Saturday, August 18, 1917, Blythe played for an army-and-navy team at Lord's against a combined Australian and South African team. It was his last match, as Blythe was killed in the Battle of Passchendaele while on active service with the British Army during World War I.

22. **Al-Ḥashāshīn** also known as **Assassins**, is the name given to the Nizari Ismailis in the mountains of Syria between about 1090 to 1275. Nizarism formed in the late 11th century after a split within Ismailism, a branch of Shia Islam. The disciples were called Asāsiyyūn (meaning "people who are faithful to the foundation). Marco Polo misunderstood the name as deriving from the term hashish, which began the myth the name Assassin derived from hash smokers. The Assassins posed a strategic threat to Sunni authority by capturing and inhabiting several mountain fortresses, including Masyaf. Asymmetric warfare, psychological warfare, and surgical strikes were often a tactic of the assassins, drawing their opponents into submission rather than risk killing them. While "Assassins" typically refers to the entire sect, only a group of acolytes known as the Fedayeen engaged in assassinations.

23. **Shaykh al-Jabal** or **"Old Man of the Mountain,"** is the name given to **Rashīd ad-Dīn Sinān** commonly referred to as **Sinān** (1137 – 1193), a missionary and a leader of the Syrian

branch of the Nizari Ismaili state (the Assassins), and a figure in the history of the Crusades. Sinān came to Alamut, the center of the Assassins, as a youth and to train as an Assassin. In 1162, the Assassin leader sent him to Syria, where he proclaimed Qiyamah, which in Nizari terminology meant the time of the Qa'im and the removal of Islamic law. Sinān based his forces in the stronghold Masyaf and controlled the northern Syria. Some ancient writings attribute him with a semi-divine status.

24. **An-Nasir Salah ad-Din Yusuf ibn Ayyub,** also known as **Saladin** was the first sultan of Egypt and Syria, and the founder of the Ayyubid dynasty. A Sunni Muslim of Kurdish ethnicity, Saladin led the Muslim military campaign against the Crusader states in the Levant. At the height of his power, his sultanate included Egypt, Syria, Upper Mesopotamia, the Hejaz, Yemen, and other parts of North Africa. Saladin eventually achieved a great reputation in Europe as a chivalrous knight because of his generosity and his fierce struggle against the Crusaders. In Dante's *Divine Comedy,* he is mentioned as one of the virtuous non-Christians in Limbo. Despite the slaughter committed by the Crusaders when they originally conquered Jerusalem in 1099, Saladin granted amnesty and free passage to all common Catholics and even to the defeated Christian army, as long as they were able to pay a ransom. (Greek Orthodox Christians were treated even better, because they often opposed the western Crusaders.) Notwithstanding the differences in their beliefs, Christian lords respected Saladin. Richard the Lionheart, King of England, once praised Saladin as a great prince, saying that Saladin was without doubt the greatest and most powerful leader in the Islamic world. Saladin is buried in a mausoleum adjacent to the Umayyad Mosque.

25. **Siege of Masyaf**. In 1176, Saladin faced a threat from the Ismaili sect known as the Assassins, led by Rashid ad-Din Sinān. Based in the an-Nusayriyah Mountains, the Assassins commanded nine fortresses, all built on high elevations.

Saladin led his army into the an-Nusayriyah range in August 1176 and besieged Sinān's castle at Masyaf. Saladin retreated the same month, after laying waste to the countryside but failing to conquer any of Sinān's forts. Viewing the expulsion of the Crusaders as a mutual benefit and priority, Saladin and Sinān maintained cooperative relations afterward, with Sinān dispatching contingents of his forces to bolster Saladin's army in a number of decisive subsequent battles.

26. **The Battle of the Somme** (July 1 – November 18, 1916) was fought by the armies of the British Empire and France against the German Empire. It took place on both sides of the upper reaches of the River Somme in France. The battle was intended to hasten a victory for the Allies and was the largest battle of World War I on the Western Front. More than three million men fought in the battle, and one million men were wounded or killed, making it one of the bloodiest battles in human history.

27. **Captain Bligh** (September 9, 1754 – December 7, 1817) was an officer of the Royal Navy. The mutiny on the *Bounty* occurred during his command of HMS *Bounty* in 1789. After being set adrift in *Bounty*'s launch by the mutineers, Bligh and his loyal men reached Timor, a journey of 3,618 nautical miles (6,700 kilometers, or 4,160 miles). **Fletcher Christian** (September 25, 1764 – September 20, 1793) was master's mate on board HMS *Bounty* during Bligh's 1787–1789 voyage to Tahiti for breadfruit plants. In the mutiny on the *Bounty*, Christian seized command of the ship from Bligh on April 28, 1789.

28. **The Tripoli War**, also known as the Turco-Italian War or in Italy as the Libyan War, was fought between the Kingdom of Italy and the Ottoman Empire from September 29, 1911 to October 18, 1912.

29. **Mechiya Oasis massacre** (October 1911), Italians attacked the population of the Mechiya oasis, killing thousands

of people, including women and children, over the course of three days.

30. **Battle of Tobruk** (1911), or the Nadura Hill Battle, was a small engagement in the Turco-Italian War.

31. **Zir'in** is a village identified as the ancient town of Yizre'el (Jezreel) mentioned by Joshua in the Bible. Yizre'el translates in Hebrew as "God give seed," from a common Canaanite root meaning to sow. Its Arabic name, Zir'in, has a similar connotation.

32. **Battle of Al-Fule** (La Fève to the Crusaders; *Castrum Fabe* in Latin), a Crusader force led by Guy of Lusignan skirmished with Saladin's army for more than a week in September and October 1183. The fighting ended on 6 October with Saladin choosing to withdraw.

33. **Möngke Kahn** was the fourth ruler of the Mongol Empire, ruling from 1 July 1251 to 11 August 11 1259. The Mongols are an East-Central Asian ethnic group native to Mongolia and China's Inner Mongolia Autonomous Region.

34. **Kitbuqa Noyan** was the leader of the Mongolian Naiman tribe, a group subservient to the Mongol Empire. He was a lieutenant and confidant of the Mongol general Ilkhan Hulagu, assisting him in his conquests in the Middle East. Kitbuqa advanced with Hulagu into western Persia, mounting a series of sieges, and commanded one of the flanks that sacked Baghdad. When Hulagu took the bulk of his forces back with him to attend a ceremony in Mongolia, Kitbuqa was left in control of Syria and the remaining Mongol army. In 1252, Möngke Khan ordered Kitbuqa to battle the fortresses of the Ismaili Nizaris. Kitbuqa assisted in the conquest of Damascus in 1260. Kitbuqa's army moved south toward Egypt and was killed at the Battle of Ain Jalut in 1260.

35. **Sultan Qutuz, or Saif ad-Din Qutuz** (d. October 24, 1260) was the third of the Mamluk sultans of Egypt in the

Turkic line. He reigned for less than a year, from 1259 until his assassination in 1260.

36. **Baibars, or Baybars**, (1228 – 1277) was the fourth sultan of Egypt in the Mamluk Bahri dynasty. He was one of the commanders of the Egyptian forces that inflicted a defeat on the Seventh Crusade of King Louis IX of France. As a commander under Sultan Qutuz, he led the vanguard of the Egyptian army at the Battle of Ain Jalut in 1260 and decisively defeated the Mongols, marking the first substantial defeat of the Mongol army. It is considered a turning point in history.

37. **The Ayyubid dynasty** was a Sunni Muslim dynasty of Kurdish origin founded by Saladin and centered in Egypt. During their relatively short tenure, the Ayyubids ushered in an era of economic prosperity in the lands they ruled, and the facilities and patronage they provided led to a resurgence in intellectual activity in the Islamic world. This period was also marked by a process of vigorously strengthening Sunni Muslim dominance in the region by constructing numerous madrasas (Islamic schools of law) in the major cities.

38. **Ain Jalut** is also known as "Spring of Goliath" or "Harod Spring." The Battle of Ain Jalut (AD 1260) was a battle between Muslim Mamluks and the Mongols in southeastern Galilee, in the Jezreel Valley, not far from the site of Zir'in. Sultan Qutuz was allied with Baibars in the face of a greater enemy after the Mongols captured Damascus.

39. **Faisal I bin Hussein bin Ali al-Hashemi** (May 20, 1885 – September 8, 1933) was king of the Arab Kingdom of Syria, or Greater Syria, in 1920, and was king of Iraq from 1921 to 1933.

40. **Waldmannsart** is a collection of centuries-old traditions and rules that a German hunter needs to follow.

41. **Major General Sir Charles Vere Ferrers Townshend**, KCB, DSO (February 21, 1861 – May 18, 1924) was a British

soldier who, in World War I, led an overreaching military campaign in Mesopotamia that led to the defeat and destruction of his command. Known as the Siege of Kut, the campaign lasted from December 1915 to April 1916 and was possibly the worst defeat suffered by the Allies during the war. After being forced to surrender, Townshend was held as a prisoner of war on Prinkipo, although he was treated like an esteemed guest, before being released in October 1918.

www.ingramcontent.com/pod-product-compliance
Lightning Source LLC
Chambersburg PA
CBHW020114180626
46812CB00006B/2601